Bluegrass Dreams Aren't for Free

A Collection of Interconnected Stories

Gerri Leen

WolfSinger Publications ⟨ Brackettville, Texas

To Walter Farley,
who many decades ago got me interested in
racing through his *Black Stallion* series.

To all the people and horses who have made racing thrilling
—and sometimes heartbreaking—
over the years, and who will continue to do so.

To Steve Haskin,
who doesn't know me, but has made me so much smarter about
horse racing with his columns and blogs and wonderful stories.

To Lisa, Paula, and Kath,
who read the first of these stories and gave me notes.

To the readers who liked the original short story
"Bluegrass Dreams Aren't for Free"
and wanted more from this universe.

To the editor who inspired this collection even though our
collaboration ultimately didn't happen.
Thank you for believing in the concept.

And to my long-departed mother and aunt,
who loved to take me to the track and didn't mind that I only
wanted to bet on the grays.

Table of Contents

Bluegrass Dreams Aren't for Free

Runaway Joe trotted down the wrong side of the huge oval Keeneland racetrack, following the other early risers onto the track. It was barely dawn, still dark enough for the clockers to find it hard to get a good look at them. For a few minutes, they'd have a little privacy as they worked on their tactics, or came back from an injury, or just did what they loved to do: run.

Joe was running early for another reason: he had things on his mind, offers from farms to consider, a life after retirement to plan —retirement that was still a long way off, but not something he wanted to leave till the last thing. Not unless he wanted to end up like his one-time rival Gray Dawn or any of the other horses who lived it up while they were winning with no eye to the future until it was too late.

In the old days, no racehorse had privacy—or free will. In the old days, some horses didn't want to run and were made to anyway with whips, drugs, medical procedures, sterilization—to get a horse's mind on the game and off mares—and whatever else the two-leggers could think of to make their investments pay off.

Most of the time it didn't matter so much what happened to the horse himself. Horses broke down; they died, right on the track. Horse racing was the only sport where an ambulance followed the players around the course.

The ambulances were still on call now, but it was the horses who did the deciding if they could walk or not. Although Joe always told his kids to listen to the vets. "Don't let pride ruin your career. If the vet tells you to get in the ambulance, do it."

Of all the two-leggers, Joe trusted the vets most. Well, after Haley, of course.

Back in the old days, two-leggers hadn't been employees or partners of racehorses like they were now, more the other way around. The horses had been the employees—if by employee you meant more like slave. Back then two-leggers had ridden on the horse's backs, whipping all the way. Joe tried to imagine what he'd do to someone who whipped him—just imagining anyone up on his back was sort of mind boggling.

He turned so he was going counterclockwise and moved faster, trot turning to canter turning to a controlled gallop. He stayed out from the rail, to let the horses really working have the inner—shorter—path around the oval. He wasn't out here to go that hard; he'd learned early in his career a near-dark track was the place he did his best thinking. Sometimes he just stood off to the side at the outside fence—his black coat blending into the early morning murkiness—and watched the others, weighing options: what race to go in next, what mares to have foals with, what his kids were up to and if he should worry about them.

In the old days, stallions went to a stud farm and made babies, and they had no choice in what mares came to them. They never saw their kids again unless the foals happened to be raised at the same farm or their sons came back as sires when they retired. No horse ever had any say in the matter.

And some horses didn't get to go to the stud or broodmare farms. Only horses who won or had impeccable bloodlines were assured that life. For the others, if they were lucky, they found a new life in show-jumping, or therapy or being a track pony for the trainer or the racetrack, or even a pasture pal for some other horse. If they were unlucky…well, two-leggers in some countries liked the taste of horse. Or they fed horsemeat to their pets.

Joe shuddered at that thought.

Things changed, at least for thoroughbreds, for good when a couple of geneticists, who were also big horse lovers, started experimenting. They knew that over time, such things as drugs and inbreeding and early retirements of less-than-sound horses had led to racehorses who were downright fragile. They began tinkering with thoroughbred DNA, adding things like goat to make the horses more nimble, a bit of cat so they'd land softer when they ran. Some squirrel for the limberness. A little bit of crow and wolf and chimp for increased ingenuity and intelligence. And then they added dolphin, and the horses started to talk.

They had a whole lot of interesting things to say, too. They were sick of things being the way they were. But they wanted to run —just under their terms, not the two-leggers.

Naturally, the old-school horse-people were not about to let genetic freaks run against "real" horses. So the hybrids ran against each other, and they didn't break down, and pretty soon their races were faster and more exciting, and the press conferences had horses taunting each other directly rather than through proxies like trainers or owners or jockeys, and it made racing super interesting for fans. It made it fun again, and two-leggers went where the racing was the most fun.

And now, hybrid racehorses were the norm, and they represented themselves as free agents—once they'd paid off their foaling fees to the farm that hosted them when they were young.

Joe had paid his fees off in record time and moved to Fairweather Farms where he'd prospered. And now he had the freedom—and resources—to plan his future, even if today didn't seem to be the day to do it. He gave up on getting inspiration from the track and walked back to the barn, cooling off as he went.

"You want a bath, Joe?" one of the track's grooms asked him.

"I'm fine." Back in the day, horses were always getting bathed. One good roll in the dirt and it was back under the hose. Foals learned at an early age that doing what came naturally was sometimes an exercise in defiance.

Not that Joe didn't love a good bath when he was hot and sweaty and maybe a little sore. But he didn't need one every time he left his stall. And he'd barely broken a sweat in the cool Kentucky morning.

As he turned into the row of barns, he could hear the sounds of horses just waking up, people getting meals ready, cats and goats and other companion animals calling to be fed.

He turned into the shedrow Fairweather Farms leased, saw Haley, and let out a low nicker.

Haley turned, his smile wide. "Hey, old man."

It was a joke between them. Haley was the old man. He'd been old when he was at Joe's mama's side when she foaled, encouraging her, then turning his attention to Joe.

The first face he'd seen. Still the first human face he saw most mornings. He thought it a handsome face, even as a few wrinkles appeared over the years and his hair lightened the same way a gray horse's did.

Joe knew Haley considered himself black but his skin was nothing like the black of Joe's coat. In horse terms, Haley would be a dark bay at best.

A dark bay who didn't have his oats ready.

"You fixed breakfast yet or you just gonna stand there admiring me?"

Haley laughed, the burst of sound making Joe happy. The track might be his favorite place to do some deep thinking but his favorite place in general was with Haley.

Haley ducked into the equipment room and came out with a bucket. Joe could tell he'd mashed the oats up just like he loved them, with maple syrup and raisins. Still he had to yank Joe's chain a little. "You didn't forget the raisins, did you, Haley?".

"No, you old coot, I didn't forget your raisins."

Joe followed him into his stall. "Good, because I wouldn't want to have to fire you over something like that."

"Like you'd ever fire me, Joe."

"You never know. Lot of people telling me they could do a better job." Sadly, true. Some people would do anything to hitch their wagon to a star. But there was no worry. Joe couldn't imagine life without Haley.

Haley poured the oats into his feeder, then leaned against the doorframe and glanced down the row of stalls. "You were up early. Big thoughts?"

"Mmmm hmmm," Joe said between bites. "Let me finish and we'll talk about it."

"Fine, I'll talk. I saw Leopard Tree in the field with Cat Drive. He's growing up to be a fine-looking colt."

Joe stopped eating long enough to say, "Stupid name. Sounds like an Appaloosa or something. He should've asked me first."

"Yeah, well, I remember your daddy saying the same thing when you picked your name."

Joe couldn't argue with that so he just focused on his oats.

"Besides, Cat Drive always likes her babies to have cat names. It's her brand, and they win, so you can't really argue with it."

Joe made a noncommittal sound. Lots of his foals had names that favored their dams. Like Miss Missive, his two-year-old filly a few stalls down. She was chestnut like her mom, Postal Lady. He'd never admit it, but Missive was one of his favorite children.

Back in the old days, stallions would never have been racing at the same time their kids were. Their whole job was to race. Once retired from the track—if they were lucky enough to be picked up by a stud farm—they just made babies. But now stallions and mares could make their own decisions. The mares could space out foals, not having to be pregnant year after year if they didn't want to. And they could still race between them if they maintained their racing form.

Stallions had it way easier, not having to carry the babies. But they had to be attractive to the mares; either through personality, or more likely, the mare thought something in the stallion's pedigree would work with something in hers to make an outstanding foal.

Not that love matches didn't happen. It just hadn't yet for Joe and he wasn't holding his breath.

"Missive's sleeping late today," Haley said as Joe finished up. "She's usually the first one awake."

"Yesterday's race took a lot out of her—I told her not to try to set the pace." Which was pretty hypocritical of him. He'd never met a race he hadn't tried to set the pace of.

"Do as I say…?"

"It's possible she's as stubborn as I used to be."

"Used to be?" Haley dodged a kick Joe didn't mean to hit him. "Well, somebody's surly—and I don't think it's about Missive's race."

"It's that Walker-Graves syndicate guy. He came back last night when you were eating—why the heck can't you eat here?"

"I got a life, too, Joe."

"You used to tell me I was your life."

"Yeah, well, maybe I have a little bit of life that's just mine." He stroked Joe's neck, as if he wanted to take any sting out of his words. "So the Walker-Graves guy…?"

"Talked my ear off about switching teams."

The thing was, it wouldn't be a bad arrangement. He'd be based near Belmont, with easy access to that track as well as Saratoga and other nearby ovals when he got a hankering to run and pick up some easy money—weren't a lot of horses could catch him.

"Walker-Graves is known for making some pretty sweet deals."

"Yeah, but I'd have to move to New York."

"Lots of good horses there. And it is 'the' city."

"Don't need a city. Doing just fine here in the bluegrass state. I'm Kentucky born, and I don't intend to leave."

"You sound just like my daddy always did—you're both a couple of diehard Kentuckians."

Joe nudged him, nestling in to grab the apple Haley always hid in his pocket—Joe *would* fire him if he ever forgot his treat.

He ate the apple happily, then meandered out of the stall to Missive's stall. She was lying down, and Joe studied her.

"What?"

"I thought she'd win." Joe's eyes were soft as he looked at his little girl. He'd spent a lot of time working with her, racing with her, the two of them flying down the backstretch as he taught her how to run—how to win.

Only not this time. It was still horse racing, after all. And there were a lot of other young horses dead set on making sure they got to the wire—and that nice freedom-buying money—first.

"Yeah, well, she probably thought she'd win, too." Haley sounded protective, which normally would have made Joe happy but today he felt cranky and wanted to argue.

Not least because she'd finished dead last, nothing left from trying to run away with the race. "She should have won. If she couldn't do that, she should have been in the money. But she didn't even finish on the board."

"Don't ride her about this. She feels bad enough as it is."

He knew Haley was right. Missive knew she'd screwed up. Her first words to him as he'd met her at the backside gate had been, "Dillinger Stables pulled their bid."

Joe hadn't even known she'd been talking to them. Dillinger Stables would have been a coup for one of his kids. That it was his favorite foal, well, that would have been even sweeter, knowing her future was so bright. That she'd lost it with one race was mighty shortsighted of Dillinger, in Joe's opinion, but maybe they'd come back once she had a chance to season.

He walked off and saw Flicker 'N Flight looking out of his stall, his eyes wary as Joe moved past him. The little bay colt was a recent free agent who'd chosen to come to Fairweather Farms. He wasn't Joe's kid; he didn't even seem to particularly like Joe. But he was really good on the track. So good he took Joe's breath away, even if he'd never admit it.

Joe knew Haley was impressed, too. He suspected his friend thought Flicker might prove even better than Joe was, but he'd never say it to his face.

"Lightweight," he muttered. Flicker was sensitive about his size, and Joe knew it.

"Relic," Flicker muttered back, stomping a little. His mane, long for a thoroughbred—in fact, he looked like a throwback to some of the Arabian foundation stallions—hung black and full. He arched his neck, looking even more exotic. No one could say he wasn't a handsome colt. But looks weren't everything.

"You think you can take me, pretty boy?" Joe knew he was all stallion, prancing with the light shining off his black coat, stern and terrible in his strength. As if he had no time for sleek young colts who were going to grow up into gorgeous stallions that might actually give him a real run.

Flicker tossed his head, as if in defiance, but ruined it by laughing a little nervously. "Like that would prove anything," he muttered, as he looked away.

Joe arched his neck in triumph, but then heard movement behind them—Missive was on her feet.

Flicker eyed her in a gentle way. "You feeling better, Missy?"

Both Joe and Haley shot him a sharp look. *Missy?*

"Watch them," Joe muttered.

"What do you want me to do?"

"What you're paid to do."

"Yeah, that seems to change daily." Haley rolled his eyes.

Joe glanced over at Missive. She hadn't answered her apparent admirer, was just looking at Joe without quite meeting his eyes. She started to fidget when he didn't light into her. "I thought I had them beat."

"You outran yourself," Flicker said gently. "I watched and you really could have held off some."

"Like you know jack about racing," Joe said, giving him a stern glance even if the colt was absolutely right. Still if anyone was going to coach his girl, it was going to be him.

"I paid my way out in record time, old man." Flicker was practically on his toes, trying to look more macho.

Joe didn't have much of an argument. Flicker *had* paid his foaling fee off in record time. He almost certainly had champion two-year-old male sewn up.

Missive shifted her weight, the nervous dance of any kid. "I'll do better next time, Dad."

Joe let go of his posturing, his tone changing as he said, "I know you will. You'll obliterate 'em next time, baby."

The tension went out of her at his words. Haley was smiling broadly. And even Flicker looked like he approved of old Joe.

Haley gave Flicker a scratch on his chin the way the colt liked it. "What do you want on your oats today, my friend?"

Flicker gave the equine equivalent of a shrug.

"Surprise you?" Haley asked gently.

Joe never liked surprises, but Flicker was a different kind of guy.

"Yeah." He was staring at Missive. "Whatever she's having."

Haley laughed and went to the feed room, and Joe followed, watching him prep the food the way Missive liked it, which wasn't all that different from the way he liked it. Acorn hadn't fallen far from the tree in this case.

"Give her extra maple," Joe said, making Haley jump. Had he not heard him behind him?

He knew he could move really quietly when he wanted to but was Haley's hearing going downhill? He'd have to be sure to make more noise around him.

"Too much maple's not good for her," Haley murmured.

"She could use some cheering up. One time won't hurt her."

"Dads and their little girls. My sis used to be able to wrap our father around her little finger, too."

"I'm not wrapped."

"Sure you are. But more maple it is."

As he worked, Joe sort of paced in front of the door.

"Something else on your mind?"

"No. Still that offer. New York."

"You take it. Or you don't. Up to you, and you know I'll go with you either way."

"But what do *you* want to do?"

"Ain't up to me, Joe."

"But if it were."

Haley took a deep whiff of bluegrass air and smiled. To Joe it smelled like green expanses, like hay, like warm, fast horseflesh. Belmont air probably smelled about the same if you were standing knee-deep in a racing barn.

"I go where you go, Joe. Where that turns out to be is up to you."

"You're not a lot of help." Joe followed him back to Missive and Flicker, mumbling something about finding a more useful employee.

Missive dug into her oats, then looked up. "Extra maple?"

"Don't thank me, girlie-girl. Your daddy gets all the credit."

"I didn't get extra maple," Flicker said, his lips pulled back in disappointment.

"And I wouldn't hold your breath till you do," Joe said, nosing Haley away from his daughter and Flicker. "Come on. We've got a racing barn to wake up."

"Smell that bluegrass." Haley took a deep whiff. "Dang, Joe. Is there a prettier place in the whole wide world?"

He breathed it in, too. "Nope. Why would we ever want to leave this?"

"So, no New York?"

"No New York." He hung his head over Haley's shoulder for a moment and pressed his cheek to his. "You'd have gone with me? Left all this behind?"

"You know it."

Joe felt safe. The way he always did with Haley.

The way he *only* did with Haley.

Why did he want to bring other two-leggers into this? Bosses and supervisors. When they could do this on their own. Couldn't they?

"Haley, good as I am, why am I still working for someone else?"

"What are you thinking?" But Haley was grinning, like he was getting it. "Our own place?"

"Yeah. Something new. A horse farm owned by an actual horse." He neighed and began to prance, suddenly nervous. But excited too.

"Lord knows you've got the money, Joe. But why start from scratch? Why not buy Fairweather Farms and rename it? Gus Abernathy is getting old, and I don't imagine he'd put up much fuss at the idea of selling the place."

"You and Gus are friends."

"Joe, *you* and Gus are friends, too. You're both just too danged surly to recognize that particular relationship."

Joe was pretty sure Haley was wrong but he liked where this conversation was going. "Feel him out. See if he'll go for it."

"You got it."

Joe liked the idea more and more. He'd be free, his kids would be safe—they'd always have a home no matter how they did on the track. And he'd end up with horses like Flicker under contract, although he'd have to be a bit nicer to the bay if he was putting money in Joe's own bank account. "It would be my legacy. To my kids."

"It would. The farm's gorgeous. A Lexington icon. Smack dab in the middle of the best horse country in the world. More than just your kids would want to live there. Think of the rent money. Think of the horses we might mentor as they come up. I think this could work, Joe."

"Being the master of my own destiny appeals." He gently nudged Haley. "As long as you're with me."

"Always."

And Down the Stretch They Come

Gray Dawn woke, got to his feet with a great deal of effort, and called for his human. Janice tended to oversleep after a late one, and she'd been out last night, celebrating a win by his daughter, Safe Haven. The pretty gray filly had gone off the favorite and hadn't let her supporters down.

Gray remembered those days. He'd quickly paid off his contract to the farm he'd foaled at and started racing for himself long before most horses ever got to. He had a cagey style of running—loved to sit back and wait for the right moment to pounce. He relied on his long stride and uncanny knack for figuring out just how much gas—so to speak—the frontrunners had in their tanks.

And then he made his move. *His* move—he'd heard tell of the old days when jockeys did the deciding but had never seen them other than on vids.

Gray could hear Safe Haven chattering with the man she'd hired on as her special assistant. Kevin did all the things you needed opposable thumbs for. And he did them loudly.

Damn, why was everything so annoying these days? Gray knew he should have retired already. Gone off to a nice farm—he'd had plenty of big stud farms wooing him—and devoted his remaining years to having fun with some very fine mares.

But he was proud. He was one of the best. Or had been. Now, he just wanted to win one last race. Even if he hadn't raced in over a year.

If he was honest, his desire to race might have something to do with Runaway Joe taunting him the other day when they'd bumped into each other—literally, big bully—in the grass the track had planted on the backside so the horses could graze.

Joe was an ass. It was bad enough he'd bought the farm he'd once worked for and turned it into a successful venture—the first owned outright by a horse. For a year now, Joe had been raking in the bucks from his own races and all the horses attached to his farm, including Flicker 'N Flight, who everyone had pegged for winning the Triple Crown this year.

Joe loved to rub Gray's face in the fact he hadn't won a race in two years. Gray saying the year off made his losing streak really only one year hadn't helped matters. Just got him called "over the hill" and "washed up."

"Might as well put you out to pasture," Joe had said, and his sleek black hide had gleamed like satin in the sunshine as he'd postured and sneered.

Gray's coat had gotten shaggy, and Janice didn't seem terribly interested in grooming him these days. But he needed to make her do it—a stallion had a reputation to uphold, a look to maintain. How else was he going to attract nice mares when he did settle down to stud? Fortunes were made, futures secured, by keeping a stallion's reputation and appearance nice and clean.

"What are you doing up?" Janice was standing at the door to his stall, rubbing her eyes.

"Get out of my way." Gray opened the stall door and pushed past her. "I'm going to jog. But I need you to get some of this excess coat off me."

"Jog? Why?" She half ran to keep up with him. "GD, hold up. What's this all about?"

"I entered myself in a race, three weeks from now—just a grade three, but it'll get me back in the game. The track was tickled to have me since I add class."

"Not if you lose. What the hell are you thinking? A graded stakes race after so much time off? You sure you don't want to start slow—maybe with an allowance?"

"Well, hell, back in the old days I could just go for a claiming race and declare myself done." He thrust his head out, trying to knock her over, but she jumped back. Even hung over, Janice was quick. "You're supposed to support me."

"I'm also supposed to help you maintain a good image. I'm a publicist, not a groom."

"You're whatever I pay you to be." He walked out to the opening of the shedrow. The cool air of an early Kentucky spring wafted to him, smelling of hot horses, liniment and bandages, but the only leather was from the straps that held the weights on for handicaps —he couldn't wrap his mind around the idea trainers used to put a bridle around a horse's head and a piece of metal in his mouth to control him. It was even more mind boggling that jockeys whipped horses—and that the horses stood for it.

If anyone took a whip to him, he'd take them for a quick ride through the rail. And maybe back again for good measure. Not that he ever let anyone on his back except for Janice's girl Deirdre. She was sweet and always brought him his favorite Gala apples. Janice brought mealy Red Delicious and thought he wouldn't know the difference.

"Mom, why are you being so mean to Gray?" Deirdre came out of a stall she was mucking out. She winked at him, and he bobbed his head the way he'd been doing since the girl first showed up on the backside and charmed him.

"I'm just being realistic." Janice sat down on a hay bale. "What's brought this on? You've had offers on top of offers for where to retire. Here in Kentucky, up in New York, down in Florida, even overseas if you want to travel."

"I'm not ready. I am ready to run." Well, ready might be an exaggeration. Ready to fall back to sleep was more like it.

"Who else is in the race?" Deirdre asked, smiling slyly. She always seemed to get what drove him, and he loved to watch his old race vids with her, explaining his strategy for each one. She knew all the horses he might compete against—and how many times he had or hadn't beaten them.

Janice rolled her eyes. "Yes, do tell."

"Good horses. I'd be slumming to go for a lesser race."

"You haven't raced in a year, and you were winless the year before."

He could feel his temper rising—something he'd inherited from his daddy. He pawed the ground, trying to work out his frustration before he said something to Janice that he'd regret.

"Mom, let me talk to him."

Janice got up and rolled her eyes again, but she left the two of them alone.

Deirdre fixed him breakfast, then went back to mucking out the stall as he ate. "New free agent coming in. Sapphira. Pretty horse. Bay with dapples." She snuck a look at him and grinned. "Not as good as a gray with dapples, obviously."

"Damn straight." Crap. Another up-and-coming young male. Just what he didn't need. "Can't wait to meet him."

"Her. Sapphir-a. That's the feminine, doofus."

Gray Dawn snorted. She was the only one he allowed to call him stuff like that, and only in private. "Well, that's okay, then. Pretty, you say?"

"Very." Deirdre reached into her pocket and pulled out an apple, then held it out, smiling as he took it very gently from her. "So who's running in the race?"

"Camelot Prince, Turnout Burnout, Runaway Joe, Santiago."

"Whoa. Runaway Joe? Are you nuts?"

"He wasn't even supposed to be entered. Didn't sign up until my name was on the roster. Jerk."

She leaned against his shoulder. "You don't have anything left to prove, Gray. Why can't you see that? The stud farms are dying for you to just pick one and get them some babies who can run. You've already proven you can do that on a small scale with your little love affairs." She batted her eyelashes, and he made the snort-whinny sound that was his version of a laugh.

"Can't help if a pretty young thing finds me attractive and wants to get in on the ground floor." Trouble was, Safe Haven was from one of his last crops. Few quality mares had been looking him up when all he did was stand around the shedrow. "I gotta race, Deirdre. The offers from the stud farms…they aren't what they used to be financially and I need to think about that. I should have snagged one when I was first eying retirement, when they were offering top dollar for me."

"So this isn't just pride? This is need? Are we in trouble?"

We. He loved that she made it them, not just him. "No, we're fine for now."

"Good."

"Yeah. But no one seems to think I've got what it takes anymore as far as racing goes. You heard your mom—and she's paid to be my biggest fan."

"Mom doesn't know shit."

"Language, young lady." He batted his nose against her to make his point. "And while your mother annoys me at times beyond measure, she's very, very good at what she does. This is a risk." He turned to eye the pasture—is that where he should be? Was he an idiot? What was the saying? No fool like an old fool.

"Fine, but Mom doesn't know anything. You're faster than all of them. You just need to train."

He knew she was right—about the training part, not the faster than anyone part, not anymore. He hadn't even been back on the track, was afraid of the clockers and all those cocky young studs looking at him in pity as he got winded running a tight quarter.

"We can go out really early." She always knew what he was thinking. "Before the others get there, when it's still dark. I'll time you." Deirdre walked over to the trunk that held the grooming items and got out the brushes and combs she needed. "And let's get you looking spiffy."

"I don't pay you to do that."

"You don't pay me to do sh—anything. I hang out here 'cause I want to." She leaned in and kissed him softly on the nose. "I love you, Gray."

"I love you, too, you little imp." He sighed in pleasure as she began to groom him. Two-leggers were essential for this. Well, they were essential if a horse was supremely lazy. Wild horses had been rolling in the dirt for centuries to shed their winter coats.

He lost himself to the feel of the shedding blade skimming off the hair at the surface, then the currycomb going deeper, then she switched to a hard brush, finally the softest one.

She combed his mane and tail, then murmured, "Doing the face now, Gray."

He just whiffed happily as she snipped his whiskers. He'd always been a sucker for a good pampering. His old groom Sally used to tell him it was the same way she felt about a massage.

"Damn, you're a fine looking horse, Gray. Nearly all white except the dapples on your rump." She kissed his nose again and he blew softly. He loved this kid, and he didn't love a whole lot of two-leggers—or four-leggers, for that matter.

She began to rub his face with a damp cloth, but then she stopped and whispered, "Oh, Gray, you're going to want to get a load of this."

He opened his eyes and saw the prettiest filly he'd ever seen—and at his age, he'd seen a lot of nice-looking females—strutting into the barn. Her coat shone so red it was almost chestnut, but her black markings made it clear she was a bay. And the dapples on her rump were a sign of glowing good health.

"Wow. The old man himself." She managed to make her voice both impressed and mocking.

Little minx. He'd seen this before in the fillies who ran against boys and routinely took them down. They were so sure of themselves. But sometimes they just needed someone a little more confident than the young bucks they were beating.

"You talking to me, youngster?"

She laughed, then seemed to notice Deirdre. Her look changed, like she hadn't imagined the venerable—and notoriously cranky—Gray Dawn hanging out with a two-legger. "Who are you?"

"I'm Deirdre. I work for Gray."

"No, she doesn't. She's my friend." He butted Deirdre hard enough to make her take a step to steady herself. "Quit saying I'm your boss."

"Okay. Didn't know you minded." She reached up and let her hand sit on his neck, the touch comforting.

"So who the hell are you?" he asked the filly, even though it was clear this could be no one but Sapphira.

"New in town." She bobbed her head in the sign of horse amusement.

"Nice. Witty repartee is great and all, but can you run?" Stupid question. She wouldn't be in this barn if she couldn't. It was quite the sought after training facility.

"Guess we'll see. I'm running against your girl in a few days."

Safe Haven was running back that fast? Did the girl never rest? Then again, she liked the money and the freedom it gave her. And Gray had a feeling she also liked that brute, Runaway Joe, and he only ever deigned to notice the highest ranked fillies and mares.

Sapphira was standing in the shedrow, looking a bit less cocky all of a sudden.

"Show her around," Deirdre whispered as she began to put the grooming tools away.

He moved closer to Sapphira. "Safe Haven is a tough one to catch."

"I know. I've already lost to her once. I can beat the boys easier than catch her."

He moved closer. "You want I should take your mind off your imminent loss to my girl by showing you the lay of the land?"

"I may not lose. But being welcomed by a living legend? I won't say no to that." She tilted her head prettily and managed to end with a low nicker that let him know she might be young, but she was definitely not immature. This was a girl who knew how to verbally tangle with a colt. Probably drove them crazy from the minute they hit the post parade to when she made them eat her dust as she passed them on the way to the wire.

But Gray was no damn colt. He ignored the mocking that might be flirting and stuck to business, showing her around, telling her she might want to rethink her first choice of stall. "You'll be last in line for chow if you take this."

"Good to know," she said as she picked a stall closer to his.

Which of course had been his intent. He felt a surge of satisfaction—confidence and a proven track record should be attractive when she thought about her offspring. Way more logical than hooking up with Mister "I set the pace, so there" Joe.

Or so he hoped. "I can show you the rest of the track. If you aren't tired from shipping here?"

"I'm game." She stayed very close to him as they explored the track. And Joe never turned up, much to Gray's delight.

It'd been a while since he'd been so captivated by a filly. Even longer since he'd felt the kind of reciprocated interest she was sending his way.

He looked good and he felt good, Deirdre would help him get ready for his race without embarrassing himself, and there was an intriguing new filly in the barn.

Life was looking up.

"How much you weigh, kid?" Gray was getting tired of running around the track in the dark with no sense of progress.

"One ten, why?"

"Get up."

"When you're training? Are you nuts?"

"Come race day, they'll pack maybe twenty pounds on Joe and I'll probably get twelve, or even less since I haven't raced. If I train with one ten, then what I do get will seem like nothing."

She leaned against him. "Gray, what if I fall?"

"I've run with you before. You've never fallen off. Get up, Deirdre. It'll be fine. Just take the weights out of the harness and you can loop your feet into that to help you stay on."

With a dramatic sigh that Gray Dawn thought only two-year-old horses and human teenagers could make, she got the weights off him and herself up and arranged. "If you kill me, Mom is going to be seriously pissed."

"It'll be awkward, that's for sure." He turned his head gently and felt her soft hands on his cheek. "Okay, hang on."

She took a strong hold of his mane. "Damn good thing I don't have to steer. Can't see for shi—I mean anything."

"Your language is atrocious. Now hit the timer and let's see how fast I can go for a half."

He knew the stopwatch she used had a light so even though it was dark out, she would be able to let him know the quarter mile splits. The white rail was easy to see in the morning murk, and it kept him true as he got used to the feel of the track under his hooves. He trotted for a moment, then moved through the canter to the gallop to his full run, staying well within himself, the way he would in a race—he never went to the lead unless there was just no pace.

When they hit the quarter pole, she called out, "Twenty-six and three."

Damn it all. In his worst race he'd managed a twenty-three flat.

He gave up trying to save anything. This wasn't a race and strategy wasn't called for. He needed to run. Fast and then faster and farther each time. The race he'd entered was a mile. If he kept on at this pace, he'd be barely in the same county by the time they hit the wire.

"Hang on," he said, and dropped down a little, the way he would when he made his run, the huge strides he was famous for taking him faster and faster, and he heard Deirdre laugh in what sounded like pure joy.

As they hit the half, he asked, "What is it?"

"Forty-eight." She patted him on the neck as he slowed. Her patting stopped as she realized how winded he was. "You okay?"

"We're going to jog some—then we go again."

"Gray, don't push."

"Something wrong with your hearing?"

She sighed. "Can't you at least do a nice slow canter? So much easier to sit than a trot."

"Fine." He took her around the track at a nice easy lope for about a mile and a half, then said, "Okay, get ready to time us again."

They hit the quarter at twenty-five and two, and the half at fifty flat.

He felt defeated and was only getting started. "Shit."

"Language, old man." She leaned down and hugged him as he walked back to where they'd left the weights. Sliding off him, she picked them up and seemed ready to carry them back to the barn.

"No, put them back in the harness."

"Seriously? Why?"

"You think I want someone—let's not call him Joe—to get the brilliant idea of putting a girl up on his back? You're my secret weapon, and secrets only stay that way when you don't advertise them."

"Also you don't want to look like a wuss who couldn't run with weights in and had to take them out and have a mere human carry them back for you."

"I will not dignify that with an answer."

She laughed as she put the weights back into their slots on the harness. "You've got plenty of time, Gray. This was great for the first time. I know you expected better, but think about it: you were carrying one ten and you'll have like a tenth of that when you race. You've got mad strategy going." She snaked her arm over his withers and they walked back to the barn in an easy—and hopeful—silence.

Gray was walking off the bath Deirdre had given him after a workout when Sapphira came out of her stall and seemed to be studying him with a serious air.

"Something on your mind, my dear?"

"What are you up to?" She apparently realized he wasn't going to stop cooling off, so she jogged a bit to catch up with him, then slowed to match his walk. "You're retired, aren't you?"

His good mood dissipated. "Who told you that?"

She gave the shake of the head that was the equine equivalent of a shrug.

"I can guess. Black, shiny, big-ass hindquarters?"

She laughed. "No. It was your daughter, dimwit. Right after she beat me by a neck."

"Oh." Crap. Had he forgotten to tell Safe Haven he was staging a comeback? He took sort of a hands-off approach when it came to his kids. They spent most of their youth with their moms, and he treated them more like buddies than beings he'd created. He knew other stallions were more involved; Joe, for one, never seemed to tire of hands-on—read: interfering—parenting.

"You thought Joe told me?"

He gave her back the head-shake shrug.

"You jealous of him?"

"Me? Jealous of *him*?"

She snort-whinnied, her walk suddenly very saucy. "Yes, of him. He is a very handsome boy."

"He's no damn boy." Was only a few years younger than him, after all.

She was quiet for a bit, and they walked along as the sun came up, and the sounds of the barns started up. Then she said, "I've always had a soft spot for grays."

He turned to look at her. "Really?" There was a world of interest in that single word, and he didn't try to hold it back.

She nudged him very gently, nose to nose, the touch making him shiver all over. "Really. Also, you like to race from behind and I like to stalk off the pace. Combining that could make for a powerful foal."

"And I can go a long time."

"Yeah, but how do you race?" Her snort-whinny made him echo her amusement with one of his own.

"You're a naughty little thing, aren't you?"

"I'm Sapphira. Take me as I am."

"Oh, I'm not complaining." He reached out to nudge her, but she danced away, another little snort accompanying the motion.

"That 'take me' part wasn't meant to be interpreted literally. A girl likes to be wooed, you know? Even if a nice gray stallion does impress the hell out of her."

She turned and pranced back to the shedrow.

He watched her the entire way.

Lord have mercy. Who the hell cared if he won the race so long as he could be close to her.

It was later than Gray liked to train when he and Deirdre got to the track.

"Two more days, Gray, and you'll be back in the starting gate."

He nodded, envisioning how the track looked through the grills, the sound of the bell as the gate doors flipped open, the sound he'd trained himself not to jump at as the frontrunners did. Getting out early had never been a priority for him—getting out cleanly was much more useful. And then being able to put himself wherever seemed the safest to make his move later. He liked to save ground by staying at the rail, but he'd run his share of risks of disqualification when a pocket opened up that wasn't quite big enough for him.

Other horses weren't shy of crying foul, and stewards didn't always go the way you thought, so he'd learned to go the outside path when it made sense. Meant he traveled longer than if he'd had a trip on the rail, but also meant he didn't interfere with anyone.

And that was fine when he was younger, when he was in tip-top shape and those extra lengths he was running on the outside didn't cost him the way they did now. He needed to get to the rail and be clever—and careful. Get through without knocking anyone around.

He could do that.

"You want me up?" Deirdre never assumed, and Gray loved her for that.

"Yep." He waited until she hopped up on his back, then jogged down the track, working the stiffness out of his legs before he really ran.

"Ready?" she asked, so in sync with him after all the days of training she could tell when he was getting set to go.

"Yep," he said, then focused on running for real.

"Twenty-three flat," she called out as he hit the quarter pole, and her voice held a note of pride that made him work even harder.

At the half he was holding steady, forty-six and one.

By the three quarter mark, he was getting tired, one eleven and four. That was okay, though. The weights had been assigned yesterday and he was at nine pounds while Joe was at twenty-two. It was insulting to Gray—showed how little of a chance the handicappers gave him—but he'd take it. And compared to the one ten he was sporting when he carried Deirdre, carrying only nine pounds was going to feel like he had wings.

By the time he hit the mile marker, going full out but tired, she called out one thirty-seven and four.

She leaned down as he galloped out, her arms around his neck. "That's great, Gray."

It was great. Compared to where they started, it was great.

But would it be good enough?

As he passed the entrance to the track, he thought he saw a black shadow standing out slightly from the murky grayness. But when he came back around again at a restrained canter, it was gone.

Gray stood at the fence near the track—the special area that never existed before horses became spectators at the races. Only humans watched back in the old day, but once the horses became the managers of their own careers—and some of the more enterprising ones became managers of the careers of their peers or kids —it became necessary to carve space out of the human viewing area and give it to the horses.

It was unusual, though, for a horse to be in the viewing area right before racing, but Gray wanted to see Sapphira's race, and since she stalked like he did—closer up than he liked to be but waited until the last minute to make her move—everything that mattered would happen at the finish line.

And it wasn't like the old days. No one needed to walk him over from the barn to the paddock, or to put a saddle on him and a piece of metal in his mouth or maybe blinkers, or tell his jockey what to do. A track official would load him up with his measly nine pounds, and it'd take him no time at all to walk from the viewing area to where the officials were stationed near the wire.

Never mind that the rest of the field were probably back in the shedrows, whispering affirmations to themselves, replaying old race vids of the other runners, or talking over final strategy with their mentors and staff.

Gray had one strategy. Well, okay, two. One: catch Joe. Two: stay clean doing it.

He was lost in thought when the crowd suddenly let out a roar. Damn it all, the race had started. It was a sprint, six furlongs on the fast dirt track, and the starting gate was on the backside chute.

But there was a big screen on the infield tote machine, and he watched as Sapphira stayed about five back in the field of eight. The quarter went down in sixteen and two—a blistering pace and Sapphira was already benefitting, moving up as the two frontrunners ran themselves out of the race, taking two stalkers who'd been lured too close to the pace with them. By the time they hit the half, they were back to a more sensible thirty-nine seconds, and Sapphira went wide even though there was room for her on the inside.

Clearly not as big a risk taker as Gray was. No way he could have resisted an open lane like that.

An open lane that suddenly closed back up when one of the pacesetters bore in, blocking any chance of getting through that way. Tiring horses usually bore out—Sapphira had obviously done her homework and watched the way her opponents raced.

But she was still mid pack as they hit the stretch. She usually ran longer races, where she would have had plenty of track left to get going. Gray wasn't sure she could finish out the way she wanted with so little room to go, but then it was like she found another gear, her strides quickening rather than lengthening as his did when he set down to run. She was a blaze of speed as she passed the tiring frontrunners and left the other closers behind.

The crowd was appreciative—she'd been co-favorite with the colt California Beacon, one of the suicidal pacesetters. As she galloped out, then turned and trotted back to the winner's circle, Gray saw Joe was also in the viewing area—when the hell had he arrived? And how dare he stare at Sapphira that way.

Joe caught Gray's eye, and his head bob was a mocking one. As he sauntered over, Joe said, "Cute gal. Hell of a runner. Even beat your girl the other day."

Safe Haven had run back quick again—too quick to Gray's way of thinking but it was her career—and she lost this time to Sapphira by a length. Gray had been in the odd position of not being sure who to cheer for. He wasn't going to share that with Joe, though. "Yep."

They stood there, not talking, both trying to pretend they didn't give a crap what the other thought or not of Sapphira, until the call to the post for the next race gave him an excuse to leave Joe standing.

But he heard the big black's hoof beats right behind him.

Sapphira was coming out of the winner's circle as they neared it, and Joe said, "Nice race. Didn't think you were going to make up the gap."

She thanked him sweetly, and Gray felt a surge of annoyance. Damn it all. Was she nice to any male?

He'd really wanted to think he was special to her.

"And what about you? No words?" She moved closer, nuzzled his neck, and murmured in his ear, "Kick his ass, okay?"

He heard Joe moving on and said, "You did great. I hope I do as well as you, how's that?"

She pulled back and seemed to be studying him, "That's pretty damn sweet. Win or lose, you're my guy, Gray." Then she touched his nose with hers and trotted back to the barn.

He wanted to watch her go, but the officials were bitching at him to quit dawdling and get weighed in. They got extra squirrely when it was a big race like this.

Oh, hell, he should just say it. When Runaway Joe—Joe, the living legend—was running. That automatically made any race a big one.

Joe—who was *not* Sapphira's guy. Gray sighed like a sappy yearling in love for the first time and it felt great.

The crowd was one of the loudest Gray had heard in a long time, clapping and cheering as he warmed up with the other horses. He'd drawn post position three in the field of five. Joe and Santiago would both want the lead. Turnout Burnout was a stalker, never more than three lengths or so off the pace. Camelot Prince was the one that ran the most like Gray, although he didn't like to be last so Gray would have that place to himself.

At least the field was small, less chance of getting into trouble —of getting himself into trouble.

The gate was in the chute, set two furlongs back from where Sapphira had started.

The horses started to load, but Joe hung back next to Gray, sticking a leg out and leaning down to bite at his knee. Or so it probably looked to the starter, since Joe was turned away from the gate as he said, "I know I've given you a lot of crap."

Gray wasn't sure where his nemesis was going with this so he stayed quiet.

"I know how hard you've trained—what you've been doing in

the mornings." He raised his head and stood straight—the perfect racehorse that the media so loved. "I'm impressed. Putting someone on your back like that. That's dedication. It won't stop me from beating you, old man, but I'm impressed."

And he did sound it.

Gray moved a bit closer. "You're only three years younger. Who you calling old?"

Joe snorted, true amusement coloring the sound. He took a step toward the gate, then looked back. "Camelot Prince is in deep financial trouble. He's willing to do anything these days to win. Watch yourself around him. Especially if you're going to try your old trick and go up the rail." He flicked his tail. "Not that you'll catch me, mind you. But I like a fair fight, and he got in the way of my girl Missive a few races back."

Missive was racing Safe Haven the following weekend. Gray had the sudden stupid thought that maybe they'd cross the line together, a dead heat.

What the hell was wrong with him? Since when did he care how Joe's kids did, especially when they were running against his own?

But he felt so mellow. He had a nice warm glow from his nemesis being so…upstanding and Sapphira seeing him off the way she had.

He better get his head in the game fast. "Thanks," he said to Joe, and trotted to the gate.

He heard someone yell, "Go, Gray!" Turning, he saw Deirdre standing by the rail. She'd already given him one hell of a pep talk before he left the barn, but clearly was going for new heights in cheering him on.

He didn't mind. It wasn't as if Joe's dignified old groom Haley was yelling for him like he was going to win the Triple Crown or something. Haley was probably up in the backside stands, where Deirdre probably should be, too. She was extra good at getting where she wasn't supposed to.

Then again, Haley had already yelled for his boss when Joe *had* won the Triple Crown. Something Gray just missed doing, killed by that extra quarter mile in the Belmont—he'd been closing but misjudged his energy level, thought he'd have more kick than he did, and managed to get within a length of the winner but that was all. Disappointed a lot of people that year—even though he'd gone on to win more races than he lost, including the Travers, the Jockey Club Gold Cup, the November Classic, and be crowned Horse of the Year. Three years later, though, Joe had done what he hadn't, and that still stung.

Deirdre was yelling her head off, her calls of "Go, Gray," carrying over the other noise of the backside.

He bobbed his head to her, then walked into his gate.

He'd barely settled when the gates flew open to the clang of the starting bell. He was grateful, not for the first time, that he wasn't one who needed to catch a flyer and get out fast. He broke slowly and went for the rail behind Camelot Prince. Santiago was in the lead with Joe sitting right off his side. Turnout Burnout was a length behind them, but the bay colt didn't look very comfortable. It was a quick pace, and Camelot Prince moved up a little as if he was afraid the others would get too far away from him.

Gray turned his own effort up a bit, feeling the lack of the hundred and one pounds now that Deirdre wasn't on his back. The weights sitting so still in the harness felt like nothing. He passed the quarter pole and started to close the distance to Camelot Prince, taking the inner route the way he liked.

And Camelot Prince bore out a little, as if inviting him to come on up.

As if inviting him...he heard Joe's words, remembered Sapphira taking the overland route. The rail was tricky because once the hole closed up, there was nowhere to go. On the outside, Camelot Prince could push him but there was a limit to how much the brown stallion would get away with before the stewards called foul, and on the outside path Gray would have a heck of a lot more room to play with.

He switched to the outside, coming fast and passing Camelot Prince before he could adjust. They hit the half-mile pole together, and then Gray was by him and running after Turnout Burnout.

He heard Camelot Prince cursing behind him, his strides picking up but not catching him.

As they rounded the far turn, Gray ducked in and caught the tiring Turnout Burnout, matching strides with him until they hit the three-quarter pole. Then he let it out.

And so did Joe. He left Santiago behind, his own strides lengthening. Gray caught Santiago mid stretch, the poor chestnut colt having nothing left after dueling for the lead with Joe.

Five lengths separated Joe and him. And then four and a half. Then three.

And that was it. They passed under the wire, Joe the winner by three lengths. Gray second by—what? He glanced back, was stunned to see the rest of the horses were at least ten lengths back.

"Nice race, old timer." Joe had slowed down as he galloped out. "But I told you there was no way you'd catch me."

"Yeah, yeah, tell me that when I'm celebrating with Sapphira."

Joe snorted, his laughter coming out a lot more pleasant than he remembered it. "She's impressive. I gotta tell you: I'm a little bit jealous."

"Yeah?"

"Yep."

"Thanks." Gray heard Deirdre yelling for him as they passed the backside, second place apparently fine with her, too.

Joe turned and led them back to the winner's circle. As they got close, he said, "I heard you're undecided on stud farms. You don't need to go to someone else's, you know? Make your own like I did. If you want advice on what not to do, I've got a ton. I think I made every mistake in the book when I started out."

Trying not to blow too much, to show how incredibly tired he was, Gray said, "Make my own?"

"Hell, yeah. Be in charge of your own destiny. Isn't that why you've never settled on one place? I know you've had a few offers."

"I've had tons of offers, kid."

"Kid." Joe snorted again. "You know where I am when you're ready. Now if you'll excuse me, I have an adoring public to go see." He swung his head, knocking him hard—harder than was probably necessary—in the neck. It probably looked like a very macho move to his adoring public. "Have fun with Sapphira."

Then he was off, and Gray turned back for the barns. This wasn't the Olympics. They didn't give medals for second and third.

They did, however, give huge wads of cash. Which would be in his accounts in a few hours. It had been a damn good day.

Deirdre and Sapphira met him at the fence to the track. Deirdre threw her arms around him and yelled in the way only a teen forgetting her dignity can, "You freakin' rocked!"

Sapphira gave him a more restrained welcome. But she was

clearly very, very pleased with him.

He escorted his two favorite girls back to the barn, Deirdre chattering happily as he and Sapphira walked shoulder to shoulder.

His own farm. Why the hell did Joe have to be smart—and actually kind of nice—as well as such a damn fine runner?

"So," he said, when Deirdre finally stopped talking, "I'm thinking of starting my own farm."

"I'll run it," Deirdre said, apparently not caring she hadn't finished high school yet.

Sapphira rolled her eyes, but it was a good-natured mocking. She seemed to like the girl. "Gonna have room for a filly like me at this farm of yours?"

"I might." He pretended to be all pumped full of "just won my first race" cockiness. "If you're really lucky."

She rolled her eyes again.

"Wrong answer?" He nuzzled her nose. "Yes, you'll get a very special spot. And I'll be the lucky one."

The Apple Never Falls Far

Safe Haven watched Missive gallop around the track, not breaking a sweat, just moving easily. There was a lot of interest in seeing the two of them meet. Money would be bet large, as Haven's handler liked to say. Haven had already beaten Sapphira, who was older and left the boys in her dust all the time; so she should be able to beat this chestnut filly who was a few months younger.

A big black horse raced up next to Missive, and Haven felt a pang—two of them actually. She had a huge crush on Runaway Joe —or Joe, as he was known around the barns—but then half the fillies did, so that wasn't unusual. But there was a different kind of feeling, watching him train with Missive, always the caring dad.

Haven didn't want to think she was jealous. Just because Gray Dawn was more a bud than a father figure shouldn't bother her. Just because he'd told some filly he had the hots for that he was coming out of retirement and forgot to tell his own daughter—that didn't make him a bad father…right?

Joe broke away from Missive and headed straight for where she was standing. "Watching the competition, Havie?"

She gave him the equine equivalent of a shrug—sometimes she envied the two-leggers' diversity of expression—and how did he know the nickname her friends used with her? Her father never called her that. "Can't hurt, right?"

"Sure can't." He watched as Missive went around another time.

"How long is she going to run?"

"She's working on endurance. Going to the front isn't a winning strategy if you can't stay there."

Haven studied him. "Why are you telling me this?"

"Because it's nothing you couldn't figure out on your own. And…I'm interested in you."

She laughed, the soft half whinny/half huff that sounded very like two-legger laughter. "That won't thrill my dad."

"I know." Joe turned to watch as a bay filly came around going blazing fast.

Sapphira. Her father's new great love. Haven relished that she'd beaten her; it shouldn't give her as much pleasure as it did, but there it was.

And the kicker was, Sapphira was really nice. Haven liked her a lot. But still, it rankled, wondering if her father had been cheering on his new girlfriend or her.

"I saw your race against her. I expected you to go for the lead, but you held back."

"I like to stalk."

"Dangerous game. Easy to get boxed in."

"Easy to get out, too, if you're patient. And not like she wasn't doing the same thing."

He conceded the point with a nod.

She took a subtle breath, taking in the scent of him. He smelled so good to her. Afraid he might think she was a lovesick idiot, she made her voice brusque as she said, "As much as I like talking to you, I've got to get on the track. I could probably stand to up my endurance too." She started to move away.

"You could train with that girl up like your dad did."

She turned back to him. "Huh?"

"Your father. To stage his comeback, he trained with that girl who's always with him up on his back. Smart."

Deirdre. Of course. Someone else her father was closer to than her. "I don't really like to emulate him." Even if she did look an awful lot like him coloring wise.

"Make your own way. I approve." He surprised her with a quick nuzzle on her shoulder, then jogged off toward the barns.

So damn handsome. And a good dad to boot. At least—if his interest held until she was older and ready to take some time off—she'd know her foal would have a dad who cared.

Missive got sick of Safe Haven stalking her around the track and headed to the pastures, where she found Flicker 'N Flight, enjoying a quick graze after training. "Hey, you."

He looked up and nickered in pleasure, mumbling "Hey, you," through a mouthful of grass.

She was too pent up to graze, and she needed to cool down, so she walked the pasture as he grazed, until he got his fill and joined her.

"So when do you leave for New York?" she asked.

"The Gotham's in two weeks. You know that."

"I do, but when do you *leave*?" She nuzzled his cheek, making him laugh.

"Friday. I want to get a chance to know the track. It's been a while since I've been in New York."

"You'll do great. You're already the favorite for the Derby. And the field doesn't look that tough."

"It won't be that easy. They've all read the early pools and they know I'm the favorite: they'll be gunning for me."

"I've seen you run, remember? They can gun all they want. You always manage to stay clear." And not by doing it her way: running to the front and staying there as long as she could, hopefully all the way under the wire. It was how her dad ran, too. She'd tried to stalk, to lay off the pace and be more patient, but it just wasn't in her nature. She loved to run and hated to let another horse get his or her head in front of her.

"Do you want to train with me this week? Before I go?" He put his head over her neck, pressing down gently. "I'm going to miss you." Then he started to laugh. "And your father will probably give my stall away while I'm gone to keep me away from you."

She lifted her head, pressing against him more tightly. "I won't let him. And you know I can get my way with him."

"I've seen it with my own eyes. Daddy's pet."

She preened a little. It was not a label she minded in the least. She heard a miaow behind her and saw her favorite cat leading a litter of kittens across the field. "Look. Matilda had her babies." She walked delicately over to the brown tabby, nosed her gently and felt a rush of happiness when the cat rose on her hind legs to rub her head against Missive's face.

Missive inspected the litter solemnly. "Very nice job on the kittens. They're going to be heartbreakers."

The cat looked over at her kittens, as if she agreed. Missive was never entirely sure if cats could understand speech or not. Inscrutable as they were, they probably could talk if they wanted to, but found it easier to rule the roost if they stayed quiet.

One of the kittens—a little black and white one—came up to Missive and swiped at her nose. Flicker pushed in, dumping him over.

Matilda, clearly not appreciating someone else disciplining her kittens, inserted herself between Flicker and the litter and gave him the look that said, "I will claw you, and you will scream like a scared foal when I'm done, if you don't cut that out."

He backed off. Missive stayed for one nose touch with a sweet little orange and white kitten, and then followed Flicker to the barns.

She had strategy to think of. Safe Haven was not going to be easy to beat and had patience on her side since she liked to stalk. Daffodil was also in the race—she'd been known to fight for the lead, causing many a front-running favorite to run herself into the ground way before the wire. Missive hadn't faced her yet, but she'd watched the replays for all the horses in the race. Daffodil won a lot.

But Missive thought she could win. Her dad seemed to think so, too—provided she kept up the stamina-building training regime he'd put her on. But she'd seen Safe Haven watching her. Her look had been weird, as if she didn't like what she saw but not in an "I'm going to lose big and there's nothing I can do about it" way. More like…contempt.

Well, Missive would just have to wipe that look off her face come Saturday.

Haven watched as her dad and Sapphira took a turn around the pasture. She rolled her eyes, then realized Deirdre had walked up and caught her doing it. "Oh, hi."

"Hey." The girl had a funny look on her face, like she thought she needed to defend Haven's dad and Sapphira or something.

"You want something, Debbie?"

"It's Deirdre."

"Right. Sorry, I have a hard time remembering the names of the help." It was mean and it made the girl's face turn red, but all Haven could think about was what Joe had said. That her dad had been training with this girl actually riding him.

And he hadn't let Haven in on it.

"Well, luckily I'm not one of your help. I work with Gray because I want to."

"Mmm hmmm, you just keep telling yourself that." She turned and left the girl standing there, ready with another retort, no doubt, but Haven wasn't about to let her use it. She walked through the barn until she found Kevin, the man she'd hired on as her manager/publicist/guy Friday.

"Princess, you look pissed as hell. What's the what?"

Kevin talked like he was in one of the gangster movies he loved so much. But he was good at what he did, and Safe Haven relaxed around his loud voice and brash attitude.

"What's your dad like, Kevin?"

"Piece of work. I take after him." He shot her a wry smile. "Seriously? The man's all right. I mean he raised me and everything, kept a roof over me and my sister, and food on the table, but I can't say we have a whole lot to talk about anymore. Not since I came over to work with you hybrids."

"He's old school?"

"He's ancient school. Decrepit school." Kevin laughed. "He races quarter horses because he doesn't like hybrids. Thinks it's a phase, even after all these years. I told him regular racing was never coming back. Did he listen? Nope. Now he's sitting on his porch wondering if he can swallow his pride long enough to get a job as a trainer with some eager, but not too picky, two-year-old hybrid."

She laughed.

"Why the sudden interest in my dad? You having daddy issues, Princess? You want I should go have a 'Come to Jesus' meeting with Gray?"

She laughed again. "Do you practice these lines?"

"Oh, toots, I've got dramatic flair. All my teachers used to tell me so." He stood. "You want a nice brushing? I'll get Martin."

"Yes, please." Martin had dreamy hands, and he sang softly while he worked—pretty songs in Spanish she barely understood but always relaxed her.

"You're not nervous about racing Missive and Daffodil, are you?"

She snorted, letting him know what she thought of that idea.

"Just checking." He got up and went down the shedrow, calling for Martin.

Footsteps sounded, two people, and she was sure it would be him with the groom, but she heard Janice's soft cough and turned to look at her.

Deirdre was standing with her mother, her face stormy.

"Someone wants to apologize to you."

"Someone doesn't need to. I know she's Gray's two-legger." Haven felt bad as soon as the words left her mouth because Janice looked so hurt at the term. The woman had always been good to her. "Listen, I'm just in a mood. Your girl caught me at a bad moment. We're fine. She can go."

Janice let go of Deirdre, who ran off with a glare she kept carefully off her face till she was behind her mom. Haven almost laughed: it's what she would have done if her father had told her to apologize to the kid.

"You okay?" Janice walked over, standing the distance most two-leggers never figured out was the right one—not so close to be threatening, not so far away to be rude. "Race jitters?"

"I'm going to win the race."

"Good. Then we'll celebrate."

Haven always liked how Janice took the time for her, even though her father was her real employer.

"I'm thinking of switching farms." It was out of Haven's mouth before she realized what she was going to say.

"Seriously?"

"Yeah." She held her head a little higher, making what she was saying sound thought out and not something she'd just decided on. "Kevin will come with me no matter where I go. And Gray won't give a shit."

Janice closed her eyes. "Actually, he will."

"Why? Because I look good for his record as a sire? I bring in more than he does at this point."

"That's true, but it's not why."

"Then why? Because he loves me and wants me nearby?" She made a half neigh, half snorting sound. Derision: that's what she was going for. At the thought her father gave a flying one about her.

"Sweetie, he does love you. He's just…a hands-off guy."

"Janice, I see you with Deirdre. I see Joe with Missive. Hands off does not equal love."

Janice took a deep breath, but she didn't seem to have a retort.

"And I didn't mean to hurt your feelings. Or Deirdre's."

Janice's smile was sweet. "I know you're hurting. I just wish I could help. But expecting GD to change is a losing proposition. I've been with him a long time."

"I know." She moved, needing to walk off the hurt this woman had no part in causing. "I'll let you know which farm I end up choosing."

"Think about this."

"Think about what?" Kevin stood in the doorway with Martin.

"She's thinking of changing farms. News to me—is it to you?"

Kevin's expression stayed the same. "She's the boss. And last I checked didn't answer to you." He gestured for Martin to go in.

"You're okay with this?"

Kevin shrugged. "I go where she goes."

Haven wanted to nuzzle him in gratitude. Until Janice walked out, and he turned to her with an angry look, "Are you out of your mind? You have a great deal here."

"So you won't come with me?"

"Of course I'll come with you. That's not the damn point. You're making an emotional decision because your dad's an asshole, and you wish you had a situation more like Missive's." At her look of surprise, he smiled grimly. "You think I just sit on my ass all day and think of funny ways to say things? I've been watching you train. You're obsessed with her and Joe. What those two have—that's never going to be how things are with you and Gray Dawn. Get over it."

Martin started to inch toward the door.

"Don't you go anywhere," Kevin said and Martin stopped. "Princess, just think about what you're doing before you make any snap decisions. We've got a hell of a good deal here. And you signed a contract for two years. There's a heavy penalty for breaking it."

She closed her eyes and shook her head, making her mane whip around. "Fine. Fine. Fine."

Kevin put his hand on her nose, stopping her movements. "Let Martin take care of you. Then we'll watch some replays. Quality time strategizing and talking shit about the competition. What do you say?"

She couldn't stay mad at him. "Fine."

He leaned in and kissed her on the nose, a daring thing to do, and one he only got away with since his expression told her he knew how close he was pushing it but just couldn't help himself. "Princess, you're the best." Then he gestured for Martin to work his magic.

It took her a while to really calm down, but once she did,

Martin's gentle touch and his pretty songs eased the tension from her body.

"I'm sorry, Miss Havie," Martin murmured softly as he worked. "I don't like to see you upset."

"Me neither," she said, making him smile and finally stop looking like he wanted nothing more than to escape her stall.

Missive was running with Flicker, enjoying how their strides were in perfect sync. It was their last day to train together and she was glad he'd been around because Safe Haven was trying to get inside her head. The gray horse had stared her down as Missive had come onto the track and seemed to be following her, a mean look on her face, until she saw Flicker was coming out.

He'd ignored her, which made Missive happy. It was bad enough her father seemed to have set his sights on this filly. She did not need her guy looking at her with any kind of interest.

"You can't let her get to you," Flicker said softly, clearly seeing way more than she gave him credit for.

"Easy for you to say. You don't have to worry about her—and Daffodil, who's probably planning on running me into the ground."

"No, I have six colts *all* planning to screw up my race any way they can." He bumped his head against hers, the way he always did when he was calling bullshit on her whining. "You don't have to take the challenge. Let Daffodil run herself into the ground. Even if it's against your nature to let anyone head you." He nuzzled her and then set off, putting an end to any discussion while they were working.

They moved away from the rail as they slowed down, finished at a nice slow canter as they went a couple more miles, both working on building up stamina. Safe Haven looked to be doing the same thing, only going slower, probably because she was on mile six or so. Missive ignored her as she and Flicker passed.

"Why does she bug you so much?"

"It's the way she looks at me. Like...I don't know how. It's weird."

"She's jealous."

"Of me? Why?"

He snorted. "Because you have a great relationship with your dad and she has almost no relationship with hers."

"That's not a new thing. Gray's never been hands on. Dad always goes on about how you can't be your foal's best bud and be an effective parent."

"Just because it's not a new thing he's absent doesn't mean she's gotten good at dealing with it. She sees you and Joe training together—that probably hurts. Maybe you should try to make nice. It's sporting and won't hurt you. The worst that can happen is she's not welcoming."

"You want me to make *friends* with her?" Missive tried to not let her lip curl but it did anyway.

"I think it might be good for both of you. I think your dad's interested in her so she may be around a lot. Plus, she hasn't got a lot of horse friends, if you've noticed."

"Well, no, if you're unpleasant, that sort of follows."

"Missy..."

She tossed her head. "Fine, fine. I'll make nice."

He nuzzled her as they dropped to a trot. "That's my girl."

Friday morning arrived, one more day before Haven planned to leave Missive eating her dust. She wolfed down the oats the grooms brought, then let Martin brush her a bit before getting ready to head for the track for her last work.

"Someone to see you, Miss Havie," Martin said, as he put his brushes away. He pointed to the door.

Missive stood there. Looking very awkward. What the hell?

"Come to spy? Trying to discover my super secret breakfast of champions recipe?"

Missive laughed, and Haven thought she really didn't want to but couldn't help it. "Mine's maple syrup in the oats."

"I don't like mine that sweet. They mix in applesauce for me."

"That sounds good, actually." Missive seemed to be shifting her weight from foot to foot. "So, I...Well, I thought maybe..."

Haven waited, not helping her out.

"Do you want to train together today?"

"Train together? What? Your boyfriend sick or something?"

"He's off to New York. As I think you know."

Haven tossed her head; she had known that, but she didn't

want to show too much interest in what this filly and her friends did.

Missive tossed her head, too. "Look, this was clearly a stupid idea. I'll see you on the track." Then she was gone, kicking up more dust than necessary.

"What the hell was that?" Kevin stood half in the stall, watching Missive as she moved away.

"She wanted to train together."

"Why?"

"Excellent question." Haven pawed the ground. "Can you load me up with double what I'm carrying tomorrow? I want to try something that apparently worked for Gray."

"Sure." He got the weight straps out and gently cinched them around her, then added the weights. "Okay?"

How much more would Deirdre weigh than this? It already felt heavy but her dad had trained with so much more.

And never told her his secret.

"It's fine. I'm going to work on stamina. I'll be a while."

"No problem. Should I be looking for new farms for us? We never did continue that conversation."

"No. Here's fine for now. I was just in a bad mood."

He nodded and patted her shoulder gently as she walked by him on her way to the track.

When she got to the track, Missive was already running, a slow gallop down the middle of the track, clearly still working on her endurance.

Safe Haven let her go by then warmed up, first an easy jog near the outer rail of the track, then she moved to the middle for a nice easy gallop. She timed it so she was even with Missive as they moved around the turn.

Missive seemed to take in the extra weight on her back and did a double take. Then she put on some speed and left Safe Haven behind.

Fine. She didn't want to run with her, either. She certainly didn't *need* to run with her. They finished their workouts nowhere near each other—Missive never bumped her speed up to get a breeze in; she seemed to have slowed as soon as she was on the other side of the track from her so they could go around without having to interact.

Fine with Haven. Things would be different tomorrow, when the gates opened. Then they'd interact for real.

Missive thought half the barns had their TVs and devices on to watch the Gotham. She stood next to her father's man, Haley and bumped him in impatience.

"Easy, little girl. Your beau is going to be on soon." He leaned in. "You ready for your race? You're cutting it a little close."

"I want to see him run."

"And I want to see you warm up. Flicker won't like it if you blow this race because of him."

She huffed and Haley shut up, holding up his hand in a way that meant, "You make your own decisions, girlie."

Her dad moved in, startling her. "Why are you still here?"

"I want to watch the race."

"Haley's recording it. Now git."

As she turned, she heard him say to Haley, "You are recording it, right? I'll never hear the end of it if you aren't."

"I wasn't going to. But I guess I am now."

Missive left, hurrying to the track, not late but not her usual punctual self. Safe Haven shot her a questioning look as she jogged past. "You almost missed the warm up."

"I know. Was busy."

"Suit yourself." She kicked up her heels and left Missive standing.

A dark horse, almost as black as her dad came jogging up. Daffodil. A hell of a big filly. One who liked to throw her weight around from what Missive had seen in the replays. "Ready to lose?"

Missive ignored her and went on with the warmup. Safe Haven was trotting back and caught up with her, saying, "I don't like her."

Missive looked at her in mystification. "Are we friends now?"

"More than we are with her. Plus she's annoying."

"And you're not?"

Safe Haven actually laughed. "Oh, I'm completely annoying, but that's not the point."

Missive realized they'd aligned their strides, were trotting prettily together toward the gate. "Look, I just want to wish you luck and a safe trip."

"Thanks. You, too."

Daffodil was waiting for them, her head curved like an Arabian. "Ah, look, it's the losers." She turned and pranced back behind the gate, probably intent on psyching out the other four horses.

"God, she's a bitch."

"Got that right. Did you watch her replays?"

Missive nodded.

"She tends to break in. Really hard. The stewards never seem to call her on it since it's at the start of the race. I know you like to catch a flyer out of the gate, but...just be careful."

"You too. You're on the other side of her. And you don't exactly break slow yourself."

"Thanks." Safe Haven seemed to let go of her normal attitude and held her head lower in a non-threatening way that for her seemed downright friendly. "Your boy's running right now, isn't he?"

"Yeah. I really wanted to see it live—you know how long it takes them to get the replays up. Haley's supposed to be recording it but he's hopeless with tech."

"Kevin's recording it. If your guy doesn't, you could come over and watch it."

"Okay. Thanks."

"Ladies, anytime," one of the officials said and they moved together toward the back of the gate.

Daffodil was already in her gate; she turned to stare at Missive as she entered, her eyes not leaving hers until the starters closed the gates behind her.

"Let's have a nice clean race," the starter said, and he seemed to be looking right at Daffodil. No way she'd risk ramming Missive now.

The gate opened, and Missive jumped out the way she loved to, anticipating the timing just right so she was moving when the doors popped open. She'd taken one step when Daffodil slammed into her, then took off into the lead.

"I told you," Safe Haven said as she found a spot behind the big black filly. "You okay?"

"I'm mad as hell."

"Well, that's what she wants. So get yourself together before you go after her."

Missive took the extra time to calm down, her need to be in

the front calling for her to run and not stay in this stalking position. She saw Daffodil seem to relax, her ears going back up, as if she thought Missive wasn't a threat.

"See ya," Missive said as she caught up with Daffodil in a few strides and then planned to burst through on the rail. A ballsy move she didn't usually have to do.

Safe Haven didn't come with her, but she didn't expect her to. She'd lay back in third and wait for the right moment. Missive put her out of her mind, intent on getting ahead of Daffodil.

Her room at the rail was getting tighter. Daffodil was bearing in slowly, forcing Missive to shorten her strides as she began to feel trapped between the larger filly and the rail.

She could imagine what her dad would tell her. "When someone pushes you, you push back. Just…don't get caught." She eased her way back out, trying to push Daffodil away and get some breathing room, but the filly was heavier than she was and didn't seem to want to move.

She was also slowing the pace down. Getting a breather.

"Oh, no, you don't," Safe Haven said, coming up fast on the outside. "No pace, no race, Daffodil." And off she went, straight to the lead before they'd even gotten down the backstretch.

Daffodil immediately went after her and Missive was free to run. She saw room at the rail, knew it could close up behind her but forced her way in. The three of them were running as one horse, and Daffodil seemed nervous trapped between them with Safe Haven not budging on the outside. They rounded the far turn, hitting the homestretch together.

Daffodil tried to kick away, but Missive put on more speed and saw Safe Haven do the same thing on the outside. Pinning her ears back, Missive gave it all she had, moving blisteringly fast, moving away from Daffodil.

But not Safe Haven. The gray filly had her ears pinned back and seemed to be taking longer and longer strides, slowly pulling away from Missive.

They flashed under the wire together, Missive's head at Safe Haven's withers. Daffodil another half length behind. The other horses in the race left well in their dust.

The "Inquiry" sign was flashing as they trotted back to the officials.

"Did you see what they did?" Daffodil's voice was shrill. "Let me talk to the stewards. I want to lodge an objection."

One of the stewards walked out. "Let's talk about the start, ladies."

Missive heard Safe Haven laugh and realized this time Daffodil might actually get her comeuppance. Although she'd only interfered with Missive, who'd still beaten her. But it was nice to watch her squirm as she tried to explain her start and the hit she'd given Missive as they left the gate, and then her little squeeze-play on the rail.

"Good race," Safe Haven said. "At the end, anyway. It was fun beating her."

"And me?"

Safe Haven shrugged. "I didn't like what she did to you. I sort of felt like we were on the same team."

"So you aren't going to remind me constantly that you beat me?"

"Nope. I'll just enjoy that I did." She snorted and went to let the officials check her weights.

Missive did the same and then waited as Safe Haven had her moment in the winner's circle. They walked back together to the barns where Safe Haven's human was waiting for them.

"Princess, you were awesome as usual."

"Princess? Is that what you go by?"

Safe Haven snorted. "I go by Havie. Only Kevin gets to call me Princess."

"Good to know."

"You recorded the Gotham, right?" Safe Haven asked. "And don't tell us who won."

"Why not?"

"Missive's got a fellow she fancies in the race."

"Ah, that handsome bay?" Kevin smiled. "Favorite in all the Derby pools? Would that be the one?"

"Yes, yes it would," Safe Haven said. She turned to Missive. "So, come watch it with us."

Missive knew her dad and Haley would be waiting for her. But she saw something on Safe Haven's face that looked a lot like loneliness. And she'd helped her during the race, going to the lead a lot sooner than she ever had before, giving Daffodil a taste of her own medicine.

"Sure. My dad doesn't like Flicker anyway. No way he'd have recorded it if it was up to him."

"I thought your dad liked everything you did, Missive?"

"Pffff." She laughed at the thought of her sire ever warning up to Flicker. "And call me Missy. It's my name with friends, not family."

"Yeah, I know how that goes. My dad never calls me Havie. But you can. If you want, I mean." Again the defensiveness arose, probably covering up what seemed like a lot of loneliness.

Flicker had been right. As usual. "Okay, Havie. Let's go see my boy trounce those other colts."

Kevin rolled his eyes. "I think you two together are going to be trouble with a capital 'T.'"

Missive laughed. "Got that right." She was always so well behaved in her own barn. Acting up a little bit over here sounded downright fun.

They watched the race, Kevin's commentary leaving Missive in stitches. The man seemed slightly insane, but he clearly loved Safe Haven.

Flicker won by three lengths.

"I can see why you like him," Safe Haven said, a bit wistfully.

"My dad likes you," Missive blurted out, then pawed the ground to try to hide how much she wished she hadn't said that.

"For real? Or just because it annoys my dad?"

"I think for real."

"That's what I keep telling her, Duchess. But does she listen to me?" Kevin leaned up against her.

"Duchess?"

"Well, she's gotta come first so you can't be a princess, too. But you're up there in my book."

Missive laughed. She thought Flicker would like this guy. Maybe she'd bring him by and show him that she'd actually done what he said, if not exactly how he'd said to do it.

Oh well, as long as it turned out okay.

When Kevin broke out the Guinness to celebrate their fine finishes and Flicker's win, she realized this might turn out to be way more than just okay.

When the Cheering Stops

Camelot Prince could hear the crowd cheering as the horses ahead of him rounded the turn. He trailed by several lengths, and no matter how fast he tried to make his legs go, he just couldn't catch up.

He'd been getting slower with each damn race. At two, he'd been a demon on the track. He'd even broken stakes records a few times. But the older he got—and he was only four—the slower he got compared to how the other horses were progressing. He could run for days, or so his manager said, but not as fast as he needed to.

Prince saw two horses ahead of him getting tired and made his legs work harder, dropping lower, trying to gain some ground. And he did. He wouldn't be last, but still, he finished twelfth in a fourteen-horse field.

There were no jeers as he went by, not like there used to be when people actually bet on him and he lost them money. Now, at thirty-to-one odds, no one was surprised he hadn't even been close to the action.

He let the officials check his weights—as if he'd still do this badly if he'd cheated? Then he jogged back to the barns.

His manager wasn't around. No shock there. Damien managed a lot of different horses, none of whom were doing all that great. When Prince had been winning, had been the precocious juvenile everyone said would be one to watch in the Triple Crown, he'd had the best two- and four-legged trainers and managers wanting to help him. Now?

He was met by an empty stall and a bored looking rat terrier who seemed to have adopted Prince as his new master. "You could probably run faster than me today," Prince grumbled at the dog, who followed him into his stall and then out again as Prince found it impossible to settle.

"Stay," Prince told the dog, as he headed off for the training track at the back of the facility. It wasn't very busy, not this late in the day, on such a warm afternoon. Prince could take the rail even though he wasn't going very fast. No danger of being run over by a horse breezing.

He looked over on his second time around the track and saw the terrier sitting next to a human he'd never seen before. Good, maybe that was the dog's person because Prince didn't need a canine. They were decent company, sure, but Prince wasn't certain he could afford to feed the dog and still pay for the manager he hardly ever saw.

He galloped on and on, letting the rhythm soothe him the way it always did. Longer races were what he needed. They used to race two miles, even more sometimes. Now, though, everyone was in love with speed.

Prince galloped for three miles and then dropped into a jog and moved to the outside of the track, the way it had been done for years, even though all the other horses were long gone off the track. Habits were ingrained: too bad the ability to win wasn't.

The man was still there, though. Petting the dog and watching as Prince came toward him.

"Unless I'm very mistaken, didn't you just run a race? Now you're jogging three miles?"

The man had kept track? What was he? Probably some reporter doing a "where are they now?" kind of story on Prince.

"Funny," Prince said, not trying to be polite. He wasn't terribly fond of two-leggers. Then again these days he wasn't terribly fond of anyone. Except maybe the damn dog now standing on his hind legs, asking Prince to touch noses.

He leaned down and let the dog lick him.

"What's his name?" the man asked.

"Haven't a clue. Take him and give him one." Prince nudged the dog toward the man.

"Isn't my dog."

"Isn't mine, either. Just showed up one day."

"Dogs are good luck to my way of thinking, boyo. Especially a loyal one like this fine thing." The man called the dog over and made a rather unabashed fuss over him. His voice rose into the range Prince usually found insulting or ridiculous, but he could tell the dog loved it. "My name is Ferguson, by the way."

"Didn't ask."

"I know, but you should have. You know what I do, Mister Camelot Prince?"

"Don't. Don't care, either."

The man huffed, just like a horse would when it was amused. Prince moved a little closer. He smelled liniment on the man. Liniment and straw and the smell of warm horses.

"You're not made for the flat, boyo."

"What am I made for, then?"

Ferguson laughed, this time a real two-legger laugh. "Steeplechase. How are you at jumping?"

Prince pawed the ground. Was this a joke? Had Ferguson heard how Prince had loved to hurdle through the fields at Academy Oaks Farms where he'd been foaled? How often he'd jumped over cars or anything else that looked challenging when he was waiting to pay off his foaling fee?

Ferguson leaned in. "You've still got a friend at your breeding farm. Remember Alison O'Brien?"

Prince thought back and recalled a young woman who'd been in charge of the gate training. "I remember her."

"She's watched your career—or lack thereof lately. She got in touch with me, told me about your penchant for leaping. And I can see you can go all day. Think you can go a mite faster and jump at the same time? But slower than flat—you don't need to set blistering fractions to win. You just have to stay on your feet over two, maybe three miles."

"And make a fool of myself losing to horses just like I do now?"

"Don't know if you're aware but the steeplechasing folk were slow to embrace you hybrid horses. You'll be getting in on the ground floor." Ferguson leaned in, a smirk evident. "There are no current hybrid stallions at stud for steeplechasing. You do well and you'll be part of the foundation. Your money issues will be a thing of the past. Maybe you'll be able to afford a name for your dog."

"He's not my dog," Prince said. But he was already thinking about what Ferguson was saying. His options on the flat tracks were limited. He'd tried grass and even the synthetic tracks that went in and out of fashion. Nothing helped. He didn't want to go work on some farm or be a trainer at the track. He wanted to race.

Hell, he wanted to win again.

Ferguson looked like he knew Prince was intrigued. "I'll pay for the move myself. You won't owe me a thing. But if you can jump the way Alison says, then you promise me that when you're a big name, you come to my stable to stand at stud. We'll be partners."

Prince studied him. "Partners?"

The man nodded. "I know you've had people—and other horses—take advantage of you, boyo. I don't mean to do that. What do you say?" He didn't hold his hand out the way a lot of two-leggers did; he leaned in: the way a horse would.

Prince leaned in, too, and let his head rest against Ferguson's for a moment, feeling a huge sense of relief at the idea that maybe, just maybe, he wasn't in this alone.

He moved back first, and Ferguson nodded and said, "Well, that's that, then." He leaned down and picked the dog up. "Why don't we name him Seamus? I had an Irish Terrier named Seamus when I was a boy."

"What does it mean?"

"It's how we say 'James' in Ireland." Ferguson smiled. "Maybe we can race there if you do really well here. That would up your stock even more."

"Don't get ahead of yourself. What happens if I don't do well?"

"Alison will take you back. She seems to have a soft spot for you, boyo. Not sure why." Ferguson winked and turned toward the stables. "Let's get you packed. We're off to Maryland."

Prince took a good look at the track, taking a deep breath of the Kentucky air. What had this place ever done for him? "I travel light. And somewhere I've got a manager I need to fire."

"Don't worry. I already did it. Not a nice man. I'm going to chalk up the slightly shady maneuvers you've been known to pull in a few of your races to his influence. I expect you to run clean, Mister."

Prince slipped into a trot so he could get to the stall first. He had no smart retort for Ferguson, primarily because the man was right: he had done some shady things to try to win.

Seamus was suddenly barking madly at his feet, keeping pace easily.

"Dumb dog. You should stick with Ferguson."

Seamus ignored him and kept on running, occasionally nipping at his heels in excitement. Prince didn't have the heart to yell at him for it.

The spot Ferguson picked to train in Maryland was lush and green, with pasture after pasture of good grass and many jumps.

"Now that they know they're welcome, hybrids are coming from all over, Prince," Ferguson said as he let down the trailer ramp. "But no one with your pedigree. Your skill, however, has yet to be determined."

Prince stepped carefully out of the trailer, getting his balance back after hours on the road. "You think I can't jump?"

"I've seen no evidence that you can. But I can wait to find out. I like surprises."

"Why wait?" Prince headed for the closest pasture. He ran past the closest jump, warming up after so long confined, letting his muscles ease and feeling the urge to fly. He turned and headed toward a jump that looked like one of the hard brushes his grooms used on him—when he could afford grooms—all bristling fibers on the top.

"Prince, it's okay to wait." Ferguson actually sounded worried.

Prince sped up, feeling his old rhythm, one he'd lost when he was racing. The number of steps, timing the takeoff, sailing over the jump, feeling the brush just kiss his ankles. He kept going, headed for the next jump and sailed over it easily.

It felt good—no, it felt great. He slowed down and cantered back to Ferguson. "Well?"

"Well, you can clearly take a jump. But can you do it in company and stay with them?"

"You're a downer, you know that? Can't we just enjoy the moment?" He heard Seamus barking madly from inside the truck. "And let my dog out."

"Oh, now he's your dog, is he?" Ferguson laughed and opened the car door, getting out of the way as Seamus leapt out. The dog ran as if he'd never seen grass before, his nose to the ground, smelling all the ways Maryland was different than Kentucky.

Prince could smell that, too. And he liked it. A lot.

"Who's the newbie?" A soft voice—a sexy voice. Prince turned to see another dark brown horse sizing him up. He'd never thought his color was particularly attractive—not as flashy as bay, not dark enough to be black—but on her it looked damned good.

"Camelot Prince."

"Ah, a high fallutin' newbie."

Prince realized the mare had the same accent as Ferguson. "You're from Ireland?"

"That I am. Here to help teach you novices."

He bristled. "I broke my maiden a long time ago."

"On the flat, you did. But you're a novice over the hedges, my dear. Although you looked quite nice a moment ago. Good form, even if your speed needs work."

"Story of my life."

She started to laugh, nodding her head up and down in a more exaggerated manner than he was used to. "It's not always good to be fast when you're jumping, Mister Prince. Just so you know. Gotta save something for the end."

"I can go all day."

"A big talker. Just what I need." She kicked her heels up at him and said to Ferguson, "You want me to get him settled in, then?"

"That'd be lovely, Branna."

Prince studied her but tried not to be too obvious about it. "That's a different name."

"Not in Ireland it's not." Again the head-nodding of amusement. "It means raven. I like ravens and crows."

He hadn't really thought about them that much.

"Why?"

"Because they're smart, they're beautiful, and they can fly." She made a face at him. "You got a problem with crows?"

"Not anymore."

She laughed, her voice sweet as she said, "Well, let's get you settled. Come on, keep up if you can." And she was off, taking a jump on the way, sailing over it in an effortless fashion that made him catch his breath. "Oh, did I not mention that I'm very good at this?" She nodded toward the next fence. "Show me what you've got, pretty boy."

She thought he was good looking? He almost messed up his timing at the thought but managed to take the jump and land handily.

"You'll do, I guess."

Seamus was following them, running around the jumps and barking crazily.

"Tell me that thing isn't yours."

"He is. His name's Seamus. He's…well, he's loyal. I'm not sure if he's bright or not, but beggars can't be choosers, isn't that the saying?"

She slowed down. "That's the saying. You planning on staying a beggar?"

He met her eyes. Maybe it was how soft they were, so at odds with her take-no-prisoners manner. Maybe it was just that he felt safe and confident for the first time in a long time. Whatever it was, it made him say, "No. I'm not."

Prince stood with Branna, watching as horses with two-leggers riding them went down the training track.

"We still share this world," he murmured, and she made a sound he thought meant disdain. "You never see this on the flat."

"No, I know. But steeplechase has always been its own world with a long tradition. That we're here at all is amazing. Fortunately, one of their traditions is to train at the break of dawn, so we can sleep in. See, off they go, back to their side of the farm."

One last horse and rider went by, and Prince stared as the man brought his crop down on the horse's flank as he urged him on down the track.

Branna looked away. "I hate that part. The two-legger that whips me will find himself a gelding straightaway."

Prince laughed but not very long. Those horses were as liable to be gelded as whipped. He couldn't imagine that happening, but Ferguson had told him it was quite common, that it made a male more tractable.

"Come on, then, they're gone and we can see how much talent you really have."

They had warmed up on the way to the track, jogging briskly, so he wasn't surprised when she set them off on a slow gallop. "Just watch me for the first two jumps as you run on the inside," she said, and he saw the jumps were set up far from the rail, leaving a clear path on the inside, so he veered off and settled in.

"It's all about the rhythm," she said. "Knowing when to jump and how to land in a way that lets you keep going. Clearing the jump isn't enough: you have to be thinking of the next jump and the next. You have to know what speed to go and how to maintain it, and how to adjust to different speeds: when you get tired and when you need to make a rush."

"Just jump already."

She did, sailing high over the jump, landing gracefully, not seeming to need to gather herself at all for the first stride as she ran on to the next jump, which she sailed over, too. Then she said, "Now your turn. Take it slow—we're not running a race today, just learning the rhythm."

He switched places with her, and then he was galloping, the first jump coming into sight, and he reached for the old knowledge, for the bone-deep sense of when to take off, how high to go, and when to relax into the landing. He cleared the fence well but it took him several awkward steps to get back into stride.

"You don't have to throw yourself up. Just sail and it'll be easier to land."

"Easy for you to say," he muttered. She was quite a bit smaller than he was. Then again, less weight might be easier to carry over the jumps but less height meant she was actually jumping higher than he was.

The next jump was coming up. When he'd been younger, he'd jumped because it felt like flying. It hadn't been work. This shouldn't be, either. He let go, leaping with less of a lurch, going lower over the fence—the hedge brushed his belly—but landing softer and not needing any extra steps to keep running.

"Perfect. Fast learner."

He took the next two with equal ease and she moved over and joined him. "You'll never be alone in a race, not unless you're a crazy pace-setter. So you need to get used to other horses doing things like this." As they leapt over the next jump, she bumped into him, and he hit the ground almost as awkwardly as his first jump.

"Hey!"

She turned her head, "What are you going to do, pretty boy? Cry foul? You'll find the stewards here are a bit less involved than on the flat. Get used to it. There's only so much jump for us all to get over: contact is going to happen."

She slowed her pace and he matched it, they took the next three jumps together, and she didn't bump him again. Then she slowed their pace even more. "All right, we're going to go for another mile if you're game?"

"I was born game."

She laughed, but they ran the rest of the way in silence, broken only by the sound of their legs and bellies rubbing against the brush on the rail, and the soft thump of graceful landings. He could feel himself falling into the rhythm of the course, a different rhythm than that of the flat racer.

By the end of the mile he was tired but not winded. "I like this."

"I can tell." She knocked her head gently against his neck. "I'll tell Ferguson that we might make a steeplechaser out of you yet."

"Only you'll leave off the 'might.'" He kicked up his heels at her and ran back to the barn.

Seamus saw him coming and ran out to meet him, then scampered along at his side as Prince walked until he was cool.

The dog barked at—well, Prince wasn't sure what he was barking at. But he was grinning in his terrier way and kept leaping at shadows until Prince stopped to take in the view.

Seamus barked again, but this time it sounded like an expression of pure happiness.

"You're right, boy. I think we're in the right place. Finally."

Branna was fussing around Prince like an old broodmare, so he knocked her away with his head. He didn't apologize when she got up in his face, clearly ready to pull her "I'm the trainer" act. "I'm ready, Branna. I've raced before."

"Never over jumps."

"And never this slow." He closed his eyes at her look. "I know, I know, it's not *that* slow if the horses are good, but it's a heck of a lot slower than flat and with lighter weights."

"And you'll be more tired because of the jumping. Don't get sloppy—or complacent." She nipped his withers, something she'd never done before.

"Are you worried? Do you think I can't do this?"

"I just—I just want you to win, all right? I'm a sentimental fool, that's what I am."

"You're the most wonderful mare I've ever been around."

"And how many have you been around, hmmm?" But her voice was pleased underneath the mocking.

"Enough to know I'm right." He moved closer. "Nuzzle for luck?"

"I'll nuzzle you all you want if you win the damn thing. Now go get on the track. And remember, there's no gate so mind what I've taught you."

He saw Ferguson standing by the fence, Seamus on a leash for once. The dog was barking madly—there was no other way Seamus barked. He was either dead asleep or freaking out over something. Prince nodded to Ferguson, told the dog to "Stay," since he wasn't sure he wouldn't try to break away and run with the field, then got in line.

It was odd not to have a gate. Odder still to have the spectators spread all around the course instead of in a grandstand. They'd only see the part of the race they were near, but Ferguson had told him it was a record crowd.

"They've come to see you, boyo."

"And Dynamic Flow and KC Boy."

"Yeah, and them, too. You three are our first big converts. It's a special day. First race for all of you." Ferguson had frowned. "Be careful. Novices can do stupid things over the jump, ruin it for you, too."

He'd promised to be careful, to watch out for those two and the other three horses running, one from Ireland and two from England.

There were no handlers to get them lined up. Just the starter, yelling at them to straighten up and race clean. Then the flag went up and Prince quickly found his rhythm, and a nice spot between the two front runners and the three laggers. Two miles he had to run, which on this track was about two and a half times around, with six fences laid out along the course. He'd jump fifteen times in all—provided he wasn't a faller. And if he wanted a nuzzle from Branna, he better not be.

This course was set up for novices. The fences were standard synthetic and brush, but they were spaced far apart, giving him ample time to find his rhythm. He'd perfected a style over the weeks he'd been training with Ferguson and Branna, skimming the fences, which she told him was bad form if he ever wanted to jump timber fences, but he'd deal with that when he got there. For now, his method worked and it kept him from expending energy he'd need later.

The strange part was hearing the crowd cheering the whole way around, not seeming to care they only saw one part of the race, giving the horses all their support in a way he'd never heard in flat racing where you got the blast of sound from the grandstand, and less bellowing cheers from the backstretch stands where the horse people usually sat, but the turns were quiet. He thought he could get used to this constant level of sound.

He realized one of the flat converts, KC Boy, was in the lead, the Irish horse behind him. Prince thought they might be having too easy a time of it and considered moving up, but he was in a safe spot right now. Jumping by himself with plenty of energy to take them on later. He let them go on and lost himself in the joy of jumping, a joy he'd never felt running flat, not even when he'd been a wunderkind.

This made him happy. Even if he ended up last, he was having the time of his life.

He glanced back to see where Dynamic Flow and the two English horses were. They hadn't moved up much so he settled in and took the fences as they came. The Irish horse seemed to be coming back to him, but KC Boy was moving out again.

"Damn it all." The pace felt off, and if Prince let KC Boy get too far ahead, there might be no catching him. The Irish horse probably wasn't used to running in this kind of heat—it wasn't that warm for Maryland, but compared to Ireland, it was hot. Branna was always complaining about the humidity and heat.

Prince passed the Irish horse, finding a new rhythm but not in time for the next jump, and he landed a little awkwardly. It took him nearly the full run to the next jump to relax, and he took that jump better.

KC Boy was only three lengths ahead. They had five jumps left —unless Prince had lost count. Branna had lectured him on keeping track—races were lost when a horse used up his energy only to find he still had fences left.

He kept his speed steady, focused on taking the next three jumps clean and sweetly, then saw that KC Boy was opening up as if in a final stretch run.

Did he not know there were two more fences? Did he not have a winning Irish mare to hound him about keeping track?

Prince saw the other horse seem to lose his stride as the next fence came into sight. He had lost track. Prince sped up slightly, hitting the fence perfectly on stride, up and over and catching KC Boy midway to the last fence.

And then passing him. He took the last fence a little crooked but still managed to land well and keep his pace, even speeding up a tiny bit as the last of the race played out like a flat. He could hear hoof beats coming fast but ignored them, content to run his own race, sure he wouldn't be caught.

One of the English horses got his head up to Prince's flank but that was as good as he could do, and the race was over.

He'd won. Finally, he'd won again.

The crowd in front of the finish line was cheering madly, and he could hear Seamus barking. Lots of other dogs were barking, too—they'd had terrier races earlier in the card. Maybe they could sign Seamus up for one of those next time.

Branna and Ferguson were waiting for him, and he thought he saw tears in the two-legger's eyes.

"I did it, partner."

"You sure did, boyo. And your first time out. You're going to keep it up, right?"

Branna nuzzled him. "He will if he wants more of this."

Seamus barked as if he was in on this, too. Prince leaned down and nuzzled the dog, felt a little choked up when the dog licked his face with great gusto. "I won, boy," he whispered. "I really won."

The dog just licked him with more gusto, like there'd never been any doubt.

Bet My Money on a Bobtailed Nag

There was a moment in a racehorse's life, that first time he crossed the finish line in front of the field. Maybe winning by a nose, maybe by lengths counted in double digits. It was a great feeling.

Or so Red Scorpion had been told. He'd never, in four years of racing, won a race. He'd never even been in the money. His best finish so far was fifth.

He still owed money on his foaling fee. More money than it looked like he'd ever earn—it had all seemed so easy when he'd been starting out. His pasture buddies had mostly gone on to pay off their fees as two-year-olds. A few didn't do it till they were three or four. But once you hit five years old and were still indentured …Red let his head hang for a moment as he took in the competition for the race he'd entered in. A maiden race, at his age. So damn embarrassing.

His odds were even more embarrassing. Forty-five to one.

Back in the old days, he'd be running in claiming races. But now that horses ran their own careers—owned themselves, other than having to pay back the foaling fee—claiming races were no more. The size of the purse showed how much was expected out of the field running. Or more accurately how much was *not* expected. Running in a race with only a thousand-dollar purse pretty much said it all.

As he loaded into the gate, he repeated the promise he'd made to himself after his last race: if he didn't finish in the money this time, he was done. No more racing.

But then what? His farm wasn't leaping up to offer him a staff job. Trainer? Pfff. Who'd want him to train them? And the farm already had a bunch of security horses—horses who'd actually won something. Not enough to pay their way free but enough to earn some loyalty.

Red was on his own and had no idea what his future held.

The gate flew open while he was still thinking. Shit. It was only a six-furlong race. He did not have time to get caught flat footed at the gate. He ran hard, trying to catch up to horses already flying, just as desperate as he was—the older ones anyway. There were a couple of youngsters—getting their first running in this level of talent would boost their confidence. Red hated that he was being used to improve a future winner's self-esteem.

He passed one of the horses in the seven-horse field, hit the turn and passed another. But the rest were out of reach. He could tell he wasn't going to catch them, even though he tried to put on more speed, to coax his legs to go faster or reach farther or whatever it was that made winners win.

He finished fifth and closed his eyes for a moment as he galloped out, then trotted back to the officials to let them check his weights.

He was done. He was done and no one but him knew it. Hell, no one but him probably cared. He went back to his stall, not spending any extra time walking off, not caring how he came out of the race.

"Better luck next time," one of the farm's grooms said.

"Right," Red said, not willing to let him in on the secret. Right—like there'd ever be a next time.

He ignored another groom who offered to bathe him, walked out of the shedrow and onto the pasture where other horses grazed or warmed up for a race.

What the hell was he going to do with his life?

"You okay?" It was a two-legger's voice. The sound less resonant than a horse's. Red had never been terribly fond of two-leggers. The ones at the farm had a way of looking at him like he'd let them down. When really he'd let himself down, not them.

He turned and saw a woman, old with white hair pulled back into a tight bun. She was wearing jeans and cowboy boots. The uniform of choice in these parts—he'd long since left Kentucky for less picky pastures. The southwest had proved ideal.

He moved closer to her. "What business is it of yours?"

She held up her hands. "Just asking. You're covered with sweat, but you're not walking. Not the thing I'm used to seeing."

He gave her the equine version of a shrug.

"I'm just saying…you seem depressed."

"And you'd know about that how?"

She smiled, and it was a smile that seemed genuine. Not the

kind he normally got from the two-leggers that said he should hurry up and go away so they could work with a winner. "I'm a psychiatrist. You know what that is?"

"Yeah." He'd been sent to one. Early in his career, before the farm wrote him off. When they cared if whatever was keeping him from winning was all in his head, if he just needed a little help getting in the game.

"Look, I'm here today recruiting. You're not the only horse I'm talking to, so don't think I've targeted you. In fact, you weren't even on my radar until I saw you brush off your groom." Something about her face told him she wasn't being entirely truthful, but he was used to two-leggers lying to him, so he didn't call her out on it.

He just turned and walked away.

She followed, until he turned and fixed her with the eye that had made many a groom back up quickly. "You stalking me?"

"I'm recruiting. Same thing only without the criminal intent." She smiled again and Red found himself responding to her energy, something in him softening even if he didn't want it to. "I'm working on a pilot program. It's for people, actually. Don't know if you know this but horses are therapeutic."

He gave a snort of disbelief.

"No, really. There are resorts where people pay tons of money just to spend hours brushing one of your not-so-self-aware brothers."

"People are idiots."

She laughed softly. "Whatever. The fact is I work with distressed youth who have been sent to my ranch to get better."

"Crazy people, you mean?"

"Not crazy. Depressed. Cut off. Isolated. That ring a bell with you? What's your name anyway?"

"Red Scorpion. And I'm not depressed."

"Well, good, since it won't do if the healer is as messed up as the patients." She moved closer. "The kids I treat need someone to talk to. Someone to take care of who isn't a person. Someone who won't judge."

"I don't like people. I'll judge the hell out of them."

She laughed again, a puff of air so strong it was almost like a horse snort. "You really don't have any filters, do you?" She held her hand up. "Never mind. Really." She started to walk away, then turned so she was walking backward. "They're looking for crowd-control horses on the police force in Dallas. The recruiter is in barn four. If you really don't like people, that should be right up your alley." Then she turned around and walked off.

He watched her go. Him, a therapy horse? Fat chance.

But crowd control? Now that sounded interesting.

Crowd control didn't sound interesting at all once Red got done talking to the police recruiter. The man had rubbed him the wrong way from the beginning of their interaction, acting like he was doing Red some huge favor by even talking to him, then going on about how much fun it was to intimidate a crowd with horses. "Although we used to have even more fun when we were the ones holding the reins." He'd said that with a straight face, as if it wasn't the most insulting thing he could say to a hybrid horse.

Red didn't like the idea of doing anything for this guy. He'd walked away while the cop was still yammering on.

He saw the woman back in the pasture later that afternoon. She was sitting under a tree, leaning against the trunk.

"Red Scorpion. How was Officer Friendly?"

"That wasn't his name."

She grinned, and Red found himself responding to her smile the same way he had earlier. "I'm Francine, by the way. Or Doctor Larned. Whichever." She closed her eyes. "You ever been to Taos?"

"I've raced all over New Mexico, but I haven't been exploring. I was a little busy." Trying to earn his way to freedom. "You should know that I still have a lot of money left on my contract."

"Does that mean you're interested in helping me?"

"Mayyyyybe."

She laughed. "Let me worry about your farm. Who should I call?"

"How do I know I won't find myself at the glue factory?" Since he was a foal, he'd heard horror stories of horses who were in bad situations and trusted the wrong two-leggers and ended up at the slaughterhouses.

"I guess you don't. I can show you pictures of the facility. The barns I've built there, the pastures we've carved out of the wilderness. But at the end of the day, it might be a lie." She dug into her pocket and held up a card. "This here says I'm certified to recruit at this and other tracks. Every recruiter here should have one or they aren't legit." She put it back in her pocket and met his eyes. "Do you think I'm lying?"

Red suddenly felt so tired. Overwhelmed by the strain of going it alone, knowing he was treading water at best, and now faced with this: trying to figure out two-leggers and their motives and whether they were lying or not. "I don't know."

She pushed herself to her feet and walked to him. "May I?" she asked as she held her hand near his face.

"Yeah."

She touched him. Not the way the grooms did, like he didn't matter, like he was just a job that had to get done. She really seemed to take her time, her palm lying gently on his cheek, then moving to his neck. "Do you like to be brushed?"

"I do." He loved it, in fact. The grooms never spent long enough on it.

"I promise you some things, Red Scorpion. I promise that if this doesn't turn out to be for you, I'll ship you back to your foaling farm on my own dime. And if it does work out, I'll buy your freedom for you, and you'll have a home with me for the rest of your life. You'll never go hungry. You'll never have to try to win a race you weren't destined to win. No one will hurt you. I give you my word." As she spoke, she kept stroking him, so slowly, so purposefully, pushing hard against his skin.

"I'm not good with people." Why was he being so honest when this was the best offer he'd had in years?

"Neither are my patients. See, one thing you have in common already."

He huffed in amusement, then said, "Okay. I'm game. How many horses are you taking?"

"Just one." She patted him on the neck and laughed. "What farm do I need to call?"

"Tequila Jack's."

She made a face. "I can't stand them."

"Something *we* have in common, then." He was gratified to see her smile. "Oh and Doctor Larned? It's just Red. My name."

"Okay, Red. Why not call me Doc? It's all western sounding."

He huffed again, but as his laughter died down, he was unsure what to do. "So, you're going to call them now?"

"Yep. Go back to your stall. I'll find you."

"Barn eight."

"Got it. I'll see you in a bit, Red."

He left her to do whatever it was that got a horse like him free from his farm. Whether he'd be free for real remained to be seen.

Red wandered out of his new barn. It was strange sharing space with mundane horses. Strange that they didn't have the run of the ranch the way he did, that they weren't allowed to explore the way he could. Larned warned him not everyone would know he was a hybrid, offered to paint a big white "H" on his rump, but he said he figured he could talk his way out of trouble.

So far no one had bothered him. Larned's ranch was well outside of Taos proper, and Red tended to do his exploring early in the morning, before it got too hot, and not that many people were up and out in the wilderness.

He always got back in time for therapy sessions. Most of Larned's patients worked with the mundane horses first. She only sent Red the ones who seemed to be needing more than the mundanes could give.

She'd sit in the straw in Red's stall while he ate breakfast and tell him the bare minimum about his next patient, explaining why she thought a particular two-legger could benefit from being around him. So far all he'd really had to do was just "be" with them. Walking around, letting them get used to his size, grazing if he was hungry. And the best part was when they brushed him. They were always taken aback the first time he corrected their technique or told them he liked something, but they seemed to get used to him talking.

And a lot of them started talking back. Telling him things he didn't really understand too much about, but Larned had told him understanding wasn't the point. Listening was, giving them someone who wouldn't hurt them or judge them or tell them how wrong they were.

The young male two-legger he had today seemed pretty much like the rest, except he had dark red hair, almost the same color as Red's liver chestnut coat. He didn't say anything about it, though. Just waited for the kid to gather up the grooming implements and follow him out to the pasture. Unlike the other horses, Red picked the spot for therapy, and today he felt like being close to the stream.

"You can talk, right?" the kid asked.

"I can." He turned to look at him. "What's your name?" Normally it didn't matter to him, but since this kid seemed to want to hold some big discussion right from the get go, they should at least know each other's name.

"What's yours?"

"I asked first."

"I'm paying to be here." The kid looked down. "Or my parents are. I didn't want to be here."

"Where did you want to be?"

The kid laughed. "You learn that from Larned? Following up with probing questions?"

"No, I just assumed if you don't want to be here, there must be someplace else you'd rather be." Red moved away, toward the far end of the pasture—the kid could catch up or not; he didn't care.

"You're supposed to be helping me."

Red turned. "Am I? Poor you, then." He trotted off, leaving the pasture through a fence Larned had shown him how to open.

"Would you wait? She's totally going to be on my case if I don't brush you."

"I'll tell her you did. Go light fires or whatever you're here for." Red heard the kid hurrying down the path after him, but first the soft click of the gate closing, like he knew to do that to keep the mundanes from escaping.

"I don't light fires. And you're kind of a dick, you know that?"

"Yeah, so I was told at the track."

"Where you lost."

"Never said I lost." Shit, had Larned told this kid Red's history?

"But you'd still be there, right? If you'd won."

"Maybe I'm just a giving kind of horse." Red slowed his pace down as he hit the rocky part of the trail that led to the stream.

"I used to run this kind of terrain. Cross country. I'm good."

"If you say so." Red walked into the stream, letting the water cool his ankles.

The kid sat down by the bank. "My name's Mark."

There'd been a few Marks. Some Toms and Steves and Zacharys too. Human names were so…limited.

"I'm Red Scorpion."

"That's a cool name. So a scorpion—I guess you're dangerous even if you're not fast."

"Faster than you." He turned to look at Mark. "I go by just Red."

"Okay." Mark started to throw pebbles gently into the water. "You special horses name yourselves, right?"

"Yep."

"Why'd you pick that?"

"It sounded cool, like you said. And my coloring."

"Being a red-head sucks." The pebbles began to fall a little harder.

"I've never found it so. But we chestnuts are pretty common in the horse world. I guess not in the two-legger world?"

"It's just one more thing people make fun of." He chucked the pebble he was holding into the woods instead of into the stream.

"There's critters in there. You could hit one. Cut it out." Red didn't really care all that much about the critters, but Mark had come a little too close to him for his liking when he tossed the last pebble. "Why are you here?" He'd never asked any of his kids that before. He figured Larned would tell him if she wanted him to know.

"Adjustment issues."

Red snorted. He'd had that at the last five tracks he'd raced at. Each stall a bit worse than the last, the food less fresh, the grooms less interested. "Been there."

"I doubt it." Mark stood. "You're just a horse."

"If you say so."

The kid met his eyes for a moment, his expression one Red was used to in mules, not in two-leggers, then Mark took off down the trail, running slow at first, but then faster.

Red glanced back at the pasture. He didn't want to follow the kid, but he'd never hear the end of it from Larned if Mark got lost. So he eased out of the stream and trotted after him, following his scent. It took him longer than he expected to catch up to the kid: he really could run.

Red ran a little behind him, not saying much unless they came to a trail fork—he was trying to keep the kid going in the general direction of "back to the ranch" and he'd discovered on his morning forays that the inner fork always looped around.

Finally, just shy of another fork that would take them to a side pasture, the kid pulled up. He leaned over, his hands on his knees, blowing heavily. "Been a while."

"You're a good runner for a two-legger."

"Yeah, it used to keep me sane." Mark laughed in a way Red didn't really understand and started to walk. When the pasture fence came into view, he said, "Can I wait to brush you tomorrow? I'm really tired."

"Yeah, that's fine. Just take the equipment back." He led Mark around the pasture fence and to the gate he could open. The bucket full of brushes and combs sat by the fence.

Mark picked it up, playing with the curry comb. "Thanks."

"For what?"

"I don't know. Running with me."

"No problem." He laughed softly. "Finally a race I can keep up in."

The kid smiled. "So you did suck at the track?"

"You could say that." He huffed, unsure why he was being so honest. Then he turned and walked off, dropping his head to graze once he'd put half a pasture between him and the boy. But he moved around so he could watch him walk back to the barn.

Not like the kid couldn't make it to the barn on his own. Not like Red was worried or…cared.

When Mark disappeared into the barn, Red finally relaxed and put all his efforts into grazing.

The next day, at breakfast, Larned said, "Mark asked if he could be assigned to you again."

"No accounting for taste."

She laughed, and he looked back at her with a shake of his head. He loved the sound of her laughter—not that he'd tell her that.

"Red, did you let him go off campus yesterday?"

"Let might be too strong a word. I left the pasture and he followed me."

"Ah. But then he ran?"

"Yeah." What was the big deal? "Is running bad?"

"Not at all." She got quiet, and he could hear her playing with the straw as she sat, the sound mingling with the crunch of his oats. "Do you like it here, Red?"

"Yep."

When he didn't say more, she laughed again and pushed herself to her feet. "Man of few words."

"Horse of few words. No need to insult me."

"Sorry. My bad." She tapped the door of his stall twice, the way she always did when their morning talks were over, and then she left.

He kept eating, enjoying the taste of the oats she'd told him were extra organic or some such thing. She was a bit of a hippie, if you asked him. But they did taste different than the ones he'd been eating at the tracks the last few years.

"Hey." It was a quiet voice, and Red turned to see Mark standing in the doorway to his stall.

"I'm eating."

"Oh, yeah. Okay." He started to turn.

"Come in and sit down. It's what all the cool kids do." Was he picking up Larned's way of speaking? Or spending too much time with these two-legged youth?

Mark laughed, the sound nothing like Larned's. Nervous and... pent up. Like a horse stuck in a shipping trailer for too long. Red knew how that felt, but he didn't see that he needed to rush through his breakfast just to make the boy feel better. He kept eating, ignoring Mark other than to listen for the sound of him getting settled in the straw, which took way longer than it needed to.

What problem was this kid here for?

The silence—broken by the sound of him chowing down— was uncomfortable at first. He could feel Mark's anxiety. But as he kept eating, Mark seemed to settle down, and the silence changed into something less highly charged.

"So, I thought maybe I could brush you in here. And then we could run again?" Mark was rustling his leg in the straw, as if he'd asked for a huge favor.

"Sure. Fine."

"I'm a good brusher. The other horses seemed to really like it."

"Great." Red wasn't sure what the kid wanted. A medal? He turned to look at Mark. "You got the equipment."

"Yeah. Just outside. I didn't want to assume anything."

Mighty decent of him. Something a horse would do, not a two-legger. "Thanks."

"Sure. No problem." The silence fell again, but it was an easy one.

Once he'd gotten every last oat, Red turned around. "Okay, so, show me what you've got, kid."

Mark stood and grabbed the bucket from outside the door. Then he got to work, and as Red felt himself being lulled nearly into a coma, he realized the boy had some serious skills.

"Told you," Mark whispered as he combed out Red's mane. "You like your tail done? Not all of the other horses did."

"Knock yourself out. You can pick my hooves while you're at it."

"Seriously? Uh—okay. I've never done that."

"I'll walk you through it. The hoof pick's out in the cabinet."

Mark went and got it and dropped it in the bucket, then went to work on Red's tail. "You're not the same red as the others."

"I'm a liver chestnut. It's darker."

"It's cool."

"I've always thought so."

Mark laughed, then went back to combing out Red's tail. When he was ready, Red walked him through the finer points of hoof picking, and it felt great having his feet done as part of the grooming. Larned usually did it for him in the evenings, when she came in to bed down the other horses.

"You don't talk a lot, do you?" Mark asked as he finished up the last foot.

"And you're a real chatterbox?"

Mark shrugged. "I guess I thought if you could talk, you'd be sort of…"

"Silly?" Red shook his head, careful not to knock into Mark. "I talk when I feel like it."

"Yeah, I get that. It's why I hate therapy. You *have* to talk or there's something majorly wrong with you."

"Well, why go if you're not going to talk?" Wasn't that like walking into a stream if you didn't want to get wet?

"Wasn't really my choice."

"Oh. Well, sorry." He gave a nice full-body shake, then said, "You wanted to run?"

"Yeah, is that okay? I mean, we were sort of told we had to stay on the ranch."

"Nobody told me that. You can blame it on me if you get in trouble." Not that he thought Mark would: Larned hadn't told him not to let the kid off the ranch when she'd known they'd been on the trails yesterday.

Red led Mark out of the barn, and they jogged to a gate near the front pasture. He opened it, let Mark out after him, and then shut it. A main road with two trails branching off lay before them. "You pick the route."

"This way." Mark was off, moving easily down the main road, and Red kept pace at his side. They didn't talk, just moved together in a rhythm that was easy to fall into.

Truth to tell, Red had never really enjoyed running on the track. But out here, in this beautiful place, he was having fun.

They went for a long time, and then Mark slowed and walked for a bit, finally stopping to take in the view. "When I first got to New Mexico, it all looked brown to me. But now I see how different it is—all the varieties."

"Where you from?"

"Seattle."

"You came a long way just to hang with horses."

Mark laughed. "Yeah, well, my parents heard Doctor Larned was good. I don't think they gave a rat's ass about the horse part." He took a deep breath. "Okay, I have no idea where we are. I hope you can get us home."

"Not a problem." It mystified him that two-leggers couldn't just follow their nose. Their scent was still fresh, leading him straight back to the ranch.

When they reached the barn, Mark stood around for a moment looking awkward. "Do you need me to do anything?"

"Nope. I'll see you tomorrow."

As Mark walked away, Red realized he was actually looking forward to more running.

They fell into a pattern. A great brushing then a long run, each time taking different routes. Some Red had never taken, but he could always find their way back by scent.

They were on a trail that seemed popular with hikers and had passed a number of them, the two-leggers looking shocked to see a boy running with a horse—the boy not riding him or leading him but simply *with* him. Red ignored them, focused on enjoying the movement and seeing the sights.

Mark finally slowed, then stopped, sipping water from a water bottle he'd slung over his shoulder in a special carrier. He poured out some water in his hand and offered it to Red, who slurped it up gratefully. Mark poured several more handfuls out for him, then put the cap back on, and slung the carrier back over his shoulder.

Red looked around, getting his bearings, and realized they were near a place people parked their cars when they wanted to hike.

As he and Mark walked, a young two-legger walked by, staring down at the phone in her hand.

"I don't understand why people walk like that. What's so interesting on that phone?"

Mark got really quiet, and Red turned to look at him. Mark shook his head, but then said, "It's like your phone is you. Without it you don't exist."

"You don't have one here yet you still exist."

"Yeah, here, but…out there. You don't know what it's like."

"Probably not." Red stopped to snack on some wildflowers he'd grown fond of.

Mark leaned against him, the contact of his back against Red's side unexpected but not unpleasant. "Do you know what texting is?"

"In concept. Structurally, I'm not really made for that kind of thing."

"Right. Yeah." Mark took a deep breath, and Red registered that it was shaky. He could feel anxiety coming off the kid in waves.

"Something you want to get off your chest?" He'd heard the head ranch hand say that to one of the guys who'd forgotten to put the regular horses' tack away.

"No." But the anxiety increased as Mark grew quiet.

"Suit yourself." Red went back to grazing.

"I was driving," Mark finally said, his voice so low Red probably wouldn't have been able to hear him if he'd been a two-legger. "My best friend was in the car with me. And I got this text from a guy I don't even like that much about this dumb party that…I don't even know why I answered." He leaned against Red more heavily.

"Or I started to answer. I never finished. I...I drove off the road, down this ravine."

"Were you hurt?"

"Yeah. I was in the hospital for a month."

"Your friend?"

"He died. The way...he hit his head on the window—that's what they said. I don't know why he had to die and I got to live when it was my fault."

Red could feel raw pain pouring into him. He wasn't sure what to do, so he just pressed back against Mark, standing very still, as the boy reached back, grabbing his mane, as if he needed something to hold on to.

"I killed my best friend, Red. There was court and some time in juvie for vehicular manslaughter. When I got out, I started skipping school. Smoking out. I stopped running. Stopped competing—I'd been all state in cross country and track but I just didn't care anymore."

"Is that why you're here?"

Again a long silence. As if Mark was trying to decide if he was going to talk. Red just waited.

"I'm here because I tried to kill myself. I took a bunch of pills. I'd had a big fight with my parents over my 'behavior,' and I just couldn't take it. They were my mom's migraine pills. God, she was pissed I'd used them up."

Red took a deep breath. "I imagine she was more scared that she'd lose you."

"Maybe." Mark pushed away from him. "I understand if you don't want to hang out with me. The kids at school—some of them have been total assholes to me. I mean I deserve it—"

"You don't deserve it. You made a mistake. Two-leggers are jerks sometimes." So were horses, for that matter. Red shook his head, not liking the emotions he was feeling but wanting to talk. "You were right when you said I sucked on the track. I'd hear the grooms sometimes. The things they'd say about me. A few 'dog food' references."

Mark turned to look at him. "It's not the same thing, Red."

"No, it's not. But it's something, right?"

Mark wiped his eyes, even though Red didn't see any tears, and said, "Can we just run now?"

"Yeah, sure."

Mark took off, running fast—as if he was trying to outrun what had happened to him. Red stayed close, being careful to not run up on his heels: he didn't want to step on him if he fell on the loose gravel. But Mark didn't fall, he just kept going, way longer than Red thought he would. Then he whispered, "Get us back?" and Red led them at a walk back to the barn. Mark collapsed in Red's stall, sitting with his arms around his legs, his head pressed down on his knees. Red closed the bottom half of the door and lay down too.

Mark finally stretched out, still staying close to the wall, and he closed his eyes.

A few moments later, Red heard his breathing change to that of sleep. He heard footsteps coming toward his stall, nickered low and the footsteps slowed. Larned peeked over the door, saw Mark there, and nodded. Then she turned and left them alone.

Red fell asleep. When he woke at the sound of the evening hay being brought in, Mark had moved closer and was lying with his hand tangled in Red's tail.

"Shhh," Red told the ranch hand carrying in the hay, glaring at him until he tiptoed and stashed the hay in the bin very quietly. "Session in progress."

Larned brought Red his breakfast herself. "I put some maple in your oats. It's organic."

"Of course it is." Red wasn't that into maple, but he didn't say so. It was nice of her and it wasn't like he disliked the stuff. "I wouldn't say no to a stout some day."

She laughed softly. "I'll keep that in mind." She leaned up against the wall next to the feeder instead of going to her normal place behind him. "You're getting through to him. He won't talk to me."

"He's talking. I don't know how much I'm helping."

"Believe me. It's helping." She stroked his neck. "I'll leave you alone." She walked out but stopped by the door. "Guinness the kind of stout you like?"

He snorted. "That'll more than do."

He was still eating when Mark came in. The kid started brushing him before he'd finished. Red decided he didn't mind and let him work. By the time Mark got to his face and hooves, he was done with his oats and feeling very relaxed from all the attention.

Mark put the equipment away, then came back in, standing at the window that looked out into the pasture. "I wish I could stay here forever."

Red didn't say anything; he didn't know what to say.

Mark finally shrugged and said, "Let's go."

They ran fast and even farther than the day before. As they walked back, Mark talked about how he'd met his best friend, then about a girl he liked—normal kid stuff, Red supposed. Except his best friend was dead and the girl he liked wasn't allowed to see him since her parents thought he was a bad influence.

Finally, he stopped and crossed his arms over his chest. "I'll always be that guy. The guy that killed his friend."

"Yeah, you will. And it's not wrong to feel bad about it, to wish things could have gone differently. Hell, you think I didn't wish I could finish in the money once in a while? I'd still be tied to that damn farm where I was born if the doc hadn't bought my freedom."

"It's not the same—"

"The hell it isn't, kid. Nobody's free. We're all tied to who we were and what we did. It's what you do now that matters. You can't take back the past. Sometimes the only thing you can do is go on." He was practically shouting at Mark and the kid stared at him, clearly surprised.

Red shook his head, frustration filling him. Why did he care about this kid? He hadn't signed up to care about him. He'd come here because here was the only place that wanted him.

"I'm sorry." Mark was rubbing his neck softly, the same way Larned had earlier. "I'm sorry. I just...I've been inside my head for so long. This—this is all I am."

"It's all you're letting yourself be. You just have to accept that you did it." Like he had to accept he was a failure of a racehorse. "And focus on things you do well. You run—for a two-legger—so beautifully. If I'd been that good, I'd still be at the track. Hell I'd probably be off living the life of a champion. Don't give that part up."

"And that sounds great. But then I see people who know what I did. I see how they look at me."

"Yeah, well, get over it. Eventually, you'll go to college, right? You'll be with people who don't know or don't care or both. But for now, you deal with it."

"It's hard."

"Yeah, kid, it is. Some of us don't get the easy road."

Mark laughed, a sharp puff of air like a horse would make, the sound a mixture of amusement and bitterness. "You're a downer."

"Like that's a surprise to you?"

Mark reached up, grabbing Red's mane as if it was some sort of lifeline, and they walked back to the barn that way. When they got to Red's stall, Mark surprised him by burying his face in Red's neck.

"It'll be okay, Mark. Just not easy."

"I get it." Mark pushed away gently. "I guess...I guess I better go talk to Larned. She's been bugging me for a session since I got here."

"Well, she's a professional, you know." Red bumped Mark gently with his nose.

"I'll see you tomorrow for a run?"

"You know where I'll be."

He watched Mark leave then moved to the door of his stall to see him walk down the row and out of the barn.

He felt a lump again in his throat and shook his head, making his mane fly. Damn it all—he'd never meant to care.

But deep down it felt really good to finally have something he could care about.

Larned showed up in the evening, a bottle of Guinness in her hand.

Red perked up as she opened it and poured it into a small tub. "Seriously?"

"Well, I'm not buying this all the time for you. But I think we should celebrate your first breakthrough, don't you?"

He slurped up the stout, sighing in happiness. He hadn't had this since he was a two-year-old, and there'd still been hope of him winning something.

"Thank you, Red," Larned said softly as he drank. "I didn't think I was going to be able to help him. I couldn't have done it without you." She rubbed his neck the way he liked.

He finished the stout and then made sure she was looking at him when he said, "No, thank you, Francine. I'm not sure what I would have done if you hadn't brought me here."

She smiled. "Well, we'll never have to find out, will we?"

"No," he said, nuzzling her gently in a way he'd never done with a two-legger. "We never will."

Running the Wrong Direction

Sapphira headed toward the track and passed Safe Haven and Missive walking off their latest race. "Which of you won?" she asked, barely slowing—she was later than she liked getting to the officials, especially for her first race on grass.

"Do you care?"

She glanced back, unsure why Safe Haven always seemed in the mood for a fight lately. "I wouldn't have asked if I didn't."

"Neither of us did. Belle Gentry nosed us both out."

"I'm sorry." She wasn't sure which filly she was apologizing to. Of the two of them, she actually liked Missive better these days. But she knew much of that was due to Gray Dawn and how Safe Haven looked at Sapphira when she was with him, like the filly was left out of her father's life because of her.

Gray was a hands-off dad. Safe Haven would feel that way no matter who was with him.

Sapphira trotted off, resolved to not think about things that weren't her business. She might be with Gray, but his relationship with his kids was entirely his affair.

"'Bout time you got here." Copperhead was prancing around the track like he owned it. Which he almost did, he'd won here so often. At least his nemesis, Stellar Song wasn't running this race, too. Sapphira wasn't sure she could beat Copperhead, let alone the two of them: they always seemed to put in a better effort when they were together than apart. "Officials are that way, young lady." He pointed with his nose, laughing at her as she cantered off.

He wasn't supposed to be in this race. She'd chosen it because most of the horses running were ones she thought she'd have a chance at beating. Then Copperhead had entered and she'd known that unless he had a really off day, she'd have to settle for second.

But that was okay. This was a test anyway. Turf purses weren't as rich—not in the states anyway—but if she could run on grass as well as she did on dirt, it would make her—and her progeny—that much more valuable when she decided to settle down.

Although Gray was talking about starting his own farm the way

Joe had. And Sapphira thought he expected her to settle down there.

She glanced over at the observation area horses used when they were just watching instead of running. There were several grays but no Gray Dawn.

He loved her. He said it all the time. But shouldn't he be here, for her first race on turf, if he loved her as much as he said?

She let the officials load up her weights then trotted down the dirt track to warm up. Copperhead joined her and seemed to be studying her.

"What?"

"Rumor is this is sort of a lark to you."

"What is?" She glanced at him. "You mean this race?"

"Yep. That you're going to retire after this."

"I'm only four."

"Yeah, well, that's the dirt I've heard. Just passing it along." He seemed to be studying her again. "So it's not true?"

"No, it's not true. And this is not a lark, bucko."

He laughed. "Okay, then. Give it your best shot, my dear." He moved off, trotting elegantly through the gap that had been opened onto the turf track.

She followed him, wanting to get a feel for the track before they loaded. It was silly, in some ways. Horses grew up running on grass: it was the first surface for just about all of them. Running on dirt, having that grit kicked back at you from the horses in front: that was the thing a horse had to get used to. Running on grass was nothing like that.

But it wasn't the surface so much as how the other horses ran on it. Sure, the grass tended toward slower fractions than dirt, but part of that was that you didn't often see serious contenders racing off with the lead and winning wire to wire. Frontrunners almost always came back to the field, and then the real racing began, down the homestretch as every horse seemed to make his or her run in the final strides of the race. The end was often a bunch of horses hitting the wire more or less together, rather than horses trailing out the way they would on dirt.

Sapphira's disadvantage was that she was a stalker. And so was everyone else. Finding the right place in the big part of the field that would lay off the lead would be crucial. She'd watched old replays with Janice, Gray's two-legger publicist, until she was so sick of them she wanted to run back to dirt.

But this was good. This was just for her. Nothing to do with Gray.

Did the other horses really think she was going to retire at four?

She was one of the last to load into the gate; she didn't want to have too much time to think while waiting for the doors to open. Her post position was toward the inside, so if she broke well, she should be able to nab a good spot and then let the race unfold as it would.

She was on her toes when the starter popped open the doors, and she was out before most of the other horses. She didn't want the lead but found herself on it, so she moved to the rail and eased up until a more experienced grass horse took the lead from her.

She could hear the others behind her, but not close. Was she going too fast? She'd be in perfect position for a race on dirt, but maybe she was going too fast for grass. She slowed a little, getting a breather, trying to pay attention to how far ahead the other horse was getting and not let the field completely run up on her.

She could tell the horses running behind her were in one big bunch. They sounded different than in a dirt race, and not just because of the grass. They were all together: she'd have to learn how to do that. This position she was in now might be no man's land.

She fought the urge to run off after the lead horse. He'd come back to them: it was how this worked. Wasn't it?

Suddenly she heard hoofbeats breaking away from the field, and a chestnut head was next to her. Copperhead took off after the lead, and she tried to run with him, willing her feet to move the way they did on dirt.

Another difference she hadn't expected. Acceleration was different. She saw Copperhead moving away with very little effort so clearly it was possible to accelerate, but it took her a few strides to get going the way she wanted to. And then she was after him.

And so were all the other horses. She was suddenly surrounded. Digging down, she found herself for a moment being left behind, and she realized Copperhead and the others ahead of her were moving a lot more lightly than she was, not digging in so much as floating over the grass.

The way she had as a foal. She quit trying so hard, let her stride come more naturally, and suddenly found herself accelerating, passing the horses who had left her a length behind. She had to weave through the field, and it was harder than it would have been in a dirt race: holes were opening and closing up much faster, but then she was clear and racing after Copperhead and the former leader, who she passed.

She couldn't get any closer to Copperhead than two lengths behind.

Second, though. On her first outing. That was good.

She caught Copperhead as they galloped out and he ran with her, then they slowed to a trot, taking the slow way back to the dirt track and the winner's circle.

"Nice race. You want some pointers on strategy? I leave tomorrow for New York but tonight I'm free—unless Gray Dawn is going to throw you a big celebration?"

She glanced at the waiting area. Still no Gray. "I'd love some pointers. Maybe while we cool down?"

"Sounds like a plan."

"So you were late getting back." Gray nuzzled her, but his words annoyed her. Did he think he owned her?

"Copperhead offered me some tips on turf."

"Good looking colt. Something I should know?" He sounded like he was trying to make it a joke, but it didn't come off very well.

"Yes. That I plan to run on grass again. It's…challenging."

"And dirt isn't?"

She moved away from him, not wanting to let his nuzzling get in the way of her thinking—or standing up for herself. "It is. But I want to be more versatile. It'll increase my value—and my foals."

He moved closer. "Our foals." He seemed to realize how that had sounded. "If I'm lucky, I mean."

"Right. If." She shook her head in frustration and could feel the celebratory braids Deirdre had put in her mane pulling. "I'm only four, Gray. I'm not retiring."

"Okay."

"No, I mean—that's what the rumor is. That I'm done. That I'm going with you to your new farm. I don't even know what it's called."

"Dawn Enterprises. I was meeting with a lawyer today."

"Is that why you didn't come to watch me?"

"Yeah. It was business. It has to come first."

"Right." She turned away, shaking her mane—how the hell was she supposed to get these braids out? They were too damn tight.

"Hey." He was nuzzling her again, something she normally loved but now was ticking her off more than anything. "Sapphira, you're young and you're on top of the world. You have no idea what it's like to not be. I've made a comeback, but I need to act now, while I'm hot again. While mares want foals with me. I found out what it's like if you wait too long."

"No. I get it. And I'm just one of those mares, right?" She shook her head again. "Where the hell is Deirdre?"

"She's at the movies."

Sapphira heard Janice at the far end of the barn. She called for her, leaving Gray alone, making Deirdre's mom take out the braids.

"Why'd you let her do this if you don't like them?" Janice asked softly, as if she didn't want Gray to hear.

"I don't know." Sapphira nickered in relief as Janice worked. It wasn't that the braids really hurt that much, but they suddenly seemed like the old leather bridles and saddles racehorses used to have to wear. Things used to…control a horse.

"I saw your race. You did good."

"It was a learning experience, that's for sure. Copperhead gave me some tips. I'll do better next time."

"About that. Someone stopped me as I was headed back here. She's from a consortium in England. She's interested in talking to you."

"About…?"

"A campaign. A few more turf races here and then…overseas. She thinks you have promise. She knows you can beat colts on dirt, and you beat all but one today. And he was champion turf horse last year, so losing to him is no ding on your record."

"And not like Gray will notice. What with his business taking off."

Janice frowned. "He'll totally notice. He loves you."

"Where was he this afternoon? Why are braids I don't even like the only celebration I got?"

"I can't answer that."

"Well, I can. He was having a meeting with his lawyer. Because business comes first."

Janice took a deep breath, the way she did when she was trying to think of the most diplomatic way to say something. "Gray was off his game for a while. Money—it could have been a problem. Now it's not, and he's enjoying that. And he's planning for a future he wasn't sure he'd have. Once he feels secure, things'll change."

"Okay." Sapphira remembered how it was when she first met Gray, how…thrilled he seemed to be that she was interested in him. And how worried he'd been that she liked Joe, his great rival.

How much of what Gray felt was love and how much was just ego? Had getting Sapphira been nothing more than a coup? Was keeping her also one?

"What's the woman's name? From the consortium?"

"Anna Leland."

"Tell her I'd like to talk to her."

Janice laughed, the sound coming out a bit sheepishly. "I already did. Meeting's tomorrow at noon."

Sapphira closed her eyes. "Thanks."

Sapphira walked out to the grazing area, looking for a two-legger who matched the description Janice had given her. She found her sitting on a fence, a long piece of grass in her mouth. She jumped down as soon as she saw Sapphira.

"Hello. Thank you for meeting with me."

"Janice told me a little about your idea. But not that much."

"It's simple really. I'm trying to bring in some new blood. I've been watching a number of you dirt horses who've been moving over to grass. To be perfectly honest, I'm most excited about you."

"Why?"

"Because you look like you can run all day. As a stalker, you can adjust to running covered up—that is: behind horses—better than one of your American speedsters who must go to the front. And you've beaten colts. Repeatedly. I like what I see."

"Thanks." Sapphira was used to praise, but the no-nonsense way this woman gave it was refreshing.

Leland tossed the piece of grass away. "Here's my plan. Two more races here, on turf, to see if this first time was a fluke or if you're taking to the surface. I'd really like to find us some more yielding tracks since our firm tracks are nowhere near as hard as yours or the Australians, and it would be good to see how you do on a little softer surface. Then, if things look good, we take you to England and train at my facility."

"Train?"

"Oh, love, if you think your tracks are challenging, welcome to my world. It's called flat racing but many of the tracks are anything but flat, they have hills and dips and odd corners. Some tracks are just one long straightaway, so they call for a different strategy if you're used to saving room at the rail or making up time on the turn. You need loads of stamina, much more than I think you've worked up here. And you'll be racing clockwise. So you'll need to work on lead changes and such. You're used to doing the opposite of what'll be called for."

Sapphira was beginning to feel a bit overwhelmed.

"I can see I'm talking too much. Don't mean to upset you, just want to be fair about what'll be expected. But you'll be racing with the elites. It's a great opportunity. Will enhance your reputation, that's for certain."

"I've always been one to do what's best for my future." Sapphira looked away and thought she saw Gray at the end of the pasture. When had he come in? "I don't necessarily want to stay in Europe forever."

"Understood. But new blood, however long it's in the program, is good. And new shooters make for more exciting races. So…are you in?"

Sapphira willed Gray to look up, to somehow know she was on the verge of making a decision that could change things for them.

He didn't.

"I'm not sure. I need to talk it over with—a friend."

Leland seemed to know who she was talking about. "We've got handsome stallions in England, too, love, for you to flirt with. You're young. Plenty of time to fall in love later."

Sapphira didn't argue with her—no need to tell her she'd already fallen in love. She just wasn't sure Gray was in love with her the same way.

"Who was the two-legger?" Gray asked her, cornering her in

her stall and making her feel very closed in.

"A trainer from England. She wants me to go there."

"Go where? Overseas?"

"Yeah."

"But...what about the farm?"

Sapphira pushed past him, getting out to the shedrow, where she didn't feel quite so corralled. "It's not always about your damn farm, Gray."

He looked taken aback. "Okay. Then what about us?"

"We can survive a separation, can't we? I mean, if you love me."

"You know how I feel. I don't want you to leave. And for what? You can race on grass here. Why go over there—unless that's where you see your future?"

"That's where I see my immediate future. The far future..." She began to paw the dirt, the way she had since she was a foal, nerves making her want to move, to do something—anything. "I guess that's up to us."

"Us—and us with me here and you thousands of miles and an ocean away?"

"Right."

"Are you leaving me?" He moved closer.

"Haven't you been listening? Yes, I'm going to England and—"

"I get that part. But me—are we done?"

"I don't know. I don't want us to be done." She let her head drop and felt him put his head over her neck. "I just don't know if we can make it when we're not together."

He didn't say anything. She was glad he wasn't full of false assurances, but she wished he could find something to say.

"It may not amount to anything if I don't win some more grass races here." She wanted to give him—them—hope.

"Okay. Sure." He looked up. "Damn it all. I forgot he was coming."

She glanced over and saw a two-legger with a briefcase. "Your lawyer?"

"Yeah. I'm sorry."

"Don't be. Business comes first."

Sapphira pranced for the crowd at Santa Anita. She was the

favorite for the Wise Dan Stakes and this time she wasn't facing either Copperhead or Stellar Song, who were busy with their own match-up in Florida. Stellar Song had beaten her two weeks ago on this very track but she'd left the other horses behind her by two lengths. Leland had been pleased.

And today was her final test. A long way from Gray and Kentucky but the sun felt good, and she was determined to enjoy it: might be a while before she felt it shine this strongly on her once she moved to England.

Leland stood by the fence, nodding at Sapphira as she walked by. Today there was no pace in the race. Sapphira could grab the lead if she was in a spot to do so. Or she could hang back off who-ever did take the lead, but she had to "mind the splits" as Leland had said. Sapphira had found out turf horses were far craftier at slowing the pace than she'd ever given them credit for. Maybe it was that dirt flew differently the faster you went, so the field wised up faster if a frontrunner tried to slow things down. On turf, there wasn't the kickback changing in intensity to show that the leader had slowed the pace to get a breather and save energy for that last mad dash to the wire.

But she was learning. And Leland had been smart. Better to learn the basics here, where at least Sapphira would still be running in the same direction and over a truly flat track, then to come to Europe a rank beginner.

Slipping through the gap in the fence, Sapphira felt the plushy grass Santa Anita worked so hard on. Her race was too long to start on the downhill part of the track, something she regretted: it would have given her valuable experience running off the flat and navi-gating a right-hand turn. She trotted by the entrance to the downhill course, now safely blocked by the outer rail, and headed to the start-ing gate.

A lot of talent in this race—this time of year the best grass races were clustered in the areas that weren't still bogged down in winter, so there were some east-coast and midwest shippers running. Sev-eral she'd beaten in her last race. She felt good—confident but not cocky. She liked running on the grass and so far it seemed like the right decision.

Even if she missed Gray a lot. But short of retiring outright, she'd have been traveling a lot this year anyway. This wasn't that out of the ordinary. Not for a young horse.

Although she'd asked Gray to come to her first race here. He'd been busy with the farm: permits or some such thing. She didn't ask him this time. Didn't want to hear whatever excuse he'd come up with for not being able to travel. So they'd settled for video chatting; Leland setting up the device on her end and Janice on his, then leaving to give them some privacy.

He'd sounded excited for her. And about his farm. Disappointed that Sapphira wasn't there to see it being built. Or maybe she was just projecting.

She forced Gray out of her mind and went into the gate, getting more on her toes than normal. If she was going to get the lead, she wanted to be out like a rocket from the gate. The others went in, everything was quiet for a moment, and the sea of green grass lay before her behind the wire slats of the gate. Then the doors flew open and she was off.

The horse next to her, a brown mare named Gentle Rain, broke just as fast and seemed to really want the lead. Sapphira let her have it but stuck close, trying to gauge the pace, listening for the announcer and just hearing him say, "The first quarter in twenty-two and two."

Too damn slow. Sapphira moved closer, lying just off Gentle Rain's weight harness, letting her know she was there and about to pass her if she didn't keep the pace honest.

Gentle Rain began to run faster, and Sapphira could tell she was annoyed at having to do it, that she'd expected to have it all her way. She bore out slightly, taking Sapphira with her. Not enough the stewards would ding her for it, but definitely making Sapphira run farther than she planned.

Deciding she might as well pass as be pushed to the outer rail, Sapphira quickened her stride and was by her and in the lead, moving to the rail as soon as she was clear of the other horse—she didn't want any possibility of a disqualification from interference.

On the lead was not where she was used to being, and it was up to her to maintain a sane pace, so she listened for the horses behind her, could hear Gentle Rain the best but soon the others were coming up—or was she coming back? She didn't feel tired, so they were probably quickening as they came around the far turn.

While she still had the room, she moved off the rail, where the grounds seemed a little soft, and stopped holding back, streaking for the wire, hearing horses coming up on her from the outside and one on the inside—Gentle Rain, who was running hard but got stuck in the softer ground, not making up the distance the way the horses on the outside were. Sapphira pinned her ears back and found another gear, running hard and ending up hitting the wire first by a nose with three horses blanketed around her.

But in turf races, this kind of finish was normal. And she'd won. Finally, she'd won.

She saw Leland nodding with a big smile as she walked by. She knew this was it, they were off for Europe. Two flights. Los Angeles to New York and then onto a different charter line for England. At least the old quarantine rules had been lifted: now horses traveled the same way two-leggers did, in and out as they pleased so long as their health records were current. It had been a fight, back in the day, but when the hybrids had refused to run anywhere quarantine was enforced, the tracks had lobbied the government, and change had ensued the way it always did when business interests collided with legislation.

Leland met her at the winner's circle. "Do you want to call Gray when we get back to the barn? Tell him you're leaving?"

Yes, she wanted to talk to Gray. No, she didn't want to tell him she was leaving.

Leland seemed to understand and stroked her lightly on the neck. "You did good. I can't wait to get you into training at my stables."

Sapphira forced a happiness she didn't feel as she said, "I can't wait, either."

Leland's stables in Newmarket were gorgeous and nothing like being stabled at the track. The barns were surrounded by acres of lush rolling countryside, and Sapphira was encouraged to run wherever she liked for as long as she liked. If she hit a white fence, she knew she'd come to the end of the property, but she didn't have to stop there. She might be stopped though since there were still a lot of mundane horses—Leland even rode one a few times when she was showing Sapphira the property—so it was not unlikely someone might ask questions if they saw her loose, not knowing if she was hybrid or mundane.

Sapphira decided to stay on the property until she got her bearings. There was more than enough room to explore.

She'd asked Leland not to come with her after they'd seen enough for her to know where to go. Mundane horses bothered her, and she knew she wasn't alone in that. Or rather, seeing them with bits in their mouths, with two-leggers astride them, bothered her. Even if Gray had trained with Deirdre on his back, that had been *his* choice, not something imposed on him.

As Sapphira trotted along, she worked on her endurance, climbing and descending hills only to find more rolling terrain in front of her, all the most brilliant green.

In the distance she saw a bay horse grazing. As she neared, he put his head up, watching her. She was pretty sure, since he was grazing with no halter on, she was dealing with a hybrid, so she said, "Hello."

"Ah, you're the American filly. Sapphira, right?" He trotted over, his movement easy.

"That's right. And who might you be?" She fell into her manner of flirting with little effort. She'd been doing it since she was foaled. Some fillies were like that, her mother had told her.

"Well, if I tell you that, then you'll have no further need of me." He moved closer. "And you might go on about your day."

"You think I'll stay just to learn your name?" She tossed her head, knowing her mane would look pretty as she did it, and trotted off.

He caught up easily. "Not one for curiosity?"

"Nope. Sorry." She eased into a canter, and he matched her stride. "But if you want to tell me your name, that's fine. Or I'll just wait till we get back to Leland's barn and check out the nametag on your stall." She shot him a look, then let her head dip a little, like a playful foal.

It had been a while since she'd flirted with anyone but Gray. It felt…strange. But fun. Not that she was looking for anything. Especially not with some horse who for all she knew monitored security at the stables. Not every hybrid was a racer.

She had a fine guy back home. She had everything she wanted back there. Even if their last conversation had been strained. He'd congratulated her on the win, but had seemed upset she was leaving.

Had he thought she was kidding?

But then he'd let it go. And she'd been upset at that. Because she wanted him to fight harder to change her mind—even though she wasn't going to change her mind. It was confusing her, all these feelings. Life was simpler when she just spent time with colts. These older stallions were so damn complicated: their issues had issues.

"You're not very interested in me, are you?" The bay moved into an easy gallop and she sped up too.

"Why do you say that?"

"I just was telling you about the best grasses and you utterly tuned me out."

"Sorry. Jetlag." Eventually that would cease to be a good excuse for everything, but she was going to milk it as long as she could. "What's your name?"

"Western Channel."

She slowed. "*The* Western Channel?"

He didn't look particularly full of himself; she'd never know he was last year's Cartier Horse of the Year just by his bearing. "Yes. *The* Western Channel. But I just go by Channel." He knocked her playfully. "Let's see you run."

And he was off. She found her stride and was after him, chasing him but not catching, up and down and around tight bends that he yelled "Mind the way," as they approached.

She and Gray had never run like this. They couldn't, not at the track. There was the pasture, which was too full of grazers to run with abandon, or the track, and going around and around was nothing like this romp across the countryside.

Finally winded, she called out, "Enough," and slowed. He eased up, his expression finally one of a champion, looking very pleased with himself.

"Hell of a workout," she managed to get out.

"We can do it again sometime if you like."

She was blowing hard and had to take a few deep breaths to finally say, "Yeah. That'd be great."

"All right then. I'll leave you to it." He stepped off the path and went back to grazing, barely breathing hard, as if he'd done nothing more than have a little jog.

She had so much work to do.

Sapphira was wandering around the farm, enjoying the serenity of being stabled nowhere near the track. She'd never thought about it, but there was an energy at the track—almost an anxiety—that was always in the background during a race meet. Horses coming and going, frantic prep happening all around, and then the highs and lows after a race. It permeated everything and she'd never realized how much more relaxed she could feel if she was away from it.

Once the meet was over, the track calmed down, but still, it was just a track. There was nowhere to explore that hadn't been seen a hundred times—or wasn't already being used by other horses who didn't appreciate you impinging on what territory they could carve out in that environment. Here everyone was on the same team. Leland and her husband were training or managing all the horses stabled at this very large farm. Sapphira could go wherever she wanted on the property and so could the other horses, although they all tended to respect each other's stalls as sacrosanct.

"Hi," Sapphira heard and turned, expecting Channel, although the voice was higher.

A bright chestnut filly was watching her. "You're the Yank."

Sapphira laughed. She'd never thought of herself as anything but a horse, but here it was clear she was an outsider, even if a fellow four-legger. "Yep. Sapphira."

The filly moved closer and Sapphira realized she wasn't even two, just big for her age. "I'm Joe's Princess." She tossed her head as if she really was a princess. "My father is Runaway Joe. Joe—you know him, right?"

"I do." Sapphira studied the filly and could see the big black stallion's influence in how rangy she was. "You're half yank, then."

"Suppose I am at that." The filly moved closer. "What's he like? I mean I've seen his race replays, so I know what he's like on the track. But my mother left the States as soon as she knew she was pregnant, and he never comes over here."

Sapphira had never known her father, either. It was common enough given the way mares chose the sires for their young. It was rarely anything more than a business decision.

She'd never really cared all that much about knowing her father. Her mother had said he had speed and that was why she'd picked him. That had been enough for her to know. But this filly clearly wanted more.

"Well, he's very handsome up close. Imposing, even. He carries himself as if the whole world should stop what they're doing and look at him." One of the reasons she picked Gray, who had seemed to look out instead of expecting everyone else to look in.

"Are you in love with him? I imagine all the fillies and mares are."

"No, I'm not in love with him, Princess. Sorry to tell you that." She moved off but the filly followed her.

"Are you in love with someone else, then? Because if not I heard Channel talking about you to our mom. I'm his sister—well, half-sister. He thinks you're pretty."

"He does, does he?" Sapphira gave herself a good shake, putting on a little bit of her own version of princess. "Actually, I've got a guy. Gray Dawn."

"My dad beats him."

Sapphira couldn't help herself. She laughed. "Yes, he does. But one of these days he might not."

"Don't think so."

"We'll see." And fortunately Joe didn't run in the same races as Gray a lot of the time, so there were still plenty of races for Gray to win. Now that Sapphira thought about it, it was almost as if the two were planning which races to run in so they didn't have to run against each other. Would Gray do that? Actually work with a stallion he obviously couldn't stand when she first met him?

If it were for the business and the farm, he probably would.

"What's it like? To be in love? My mother never has been—or so she tells me." Princess was following along as if Sapphira was her new best friend.

"It's wonderful." Or it had been until she started wondering if her stallion really loved her.

"You don't sound very happy."

"I'm lonely. Missing him. He's in Kentucky and I'm here."

"That makes sense." The filly moved closer. "Do you want to gallop with me? I'm supposed to go easy till I get through this growth spurt, so I thought you'd be a good running partner."

Sapphira laughed again. "You do realize you just insulted me, right?"

Princess actually looked embarrassed. "Sorry. I'm a bit blunt."

"Just a bit?" Sapphira knocked her gently with her head. "All right. Slum away." She could use the workout.

"Does that mean yes?"

"Come on and run." Sapphira trotted off, not worrying if Princess would catch up. She was Channel's sister. She'd probably end up in front.

But not for much longer. Sapphira was already so much better than she'd been during that first run with Channel. Stronger and more nimble. Learning how to pace herself for both the uphill push and to taper off for the downhill coasts. Getting used to softer ground, too. Harder to run on in some ways, but so much more forgiving on hooves and legs.

She was making a mental list of things to tell Gray about this place the next time they talked. So many ways he could make his farm like this—a place where horses could really excel, and also enjoy themselves.

She couldn't wait until their next video chat.

Sapphira trotted off the track at Newmarket, toward the waiting van. Leland was looking at her phone and held it up as she approached. "Nice purse for your first outing. I was pleased. How did you feel?"

"I'm still a little shaky on the lead changes. It's just so automatic to do it for running the other direction and with turns."

"You'll get used to it. And if you have to think about it, that's okay. Keeps you present. What about the surface? Any problems?"

"I won, didn't I?"

Leland laughed. "Don't get uppity, love."

"I still need to work on my ascents. I slowed down more than the other horses did. I really came back to the field." And she'd been stalking behind two horses on the lead who hadn't come back, not until the stretch.

"Yeah, that's what I noticed, too. I'll get Channel to work with you on that."

"I did okay, though, right?" She hated how tentative she sounded: she'd just won for God's sake. Against veteran English fillies and mares.

"You were brilliant. We'll celebrate when we get back to the stables. Now go walk off the race for a while. I don't want you cramping up on the way back home."

Sapphira walked it off, passing by Leland occasionally and she would read comments about her race from social media. With each pass, Sapphira felt better and better about the race.

When she was good and cool, she headed for the van door, and one of the grooms let her in. The ride was short, and she exited the van to find Princess waiting.

The chestnut danced around her, nuzzling her in excitement. "I knew once you started beating me that you'd win."

"Nothing wrong with your ego, kiddo."

Princess just laughed. Channel was waiting by Sapphira's stall, where her favorite apples had been laid out.

"Nice race," Sapphira said to him. He'd run earlier in a Group 3 race—much tougher company than what she'd faced, but slumming for him. It had been his first start since last year's winning campaign; he'd move up to a Group 1 race next, no doubt.

"And I return the compliment. I think you're going to do famously here."

She shook her mane, unable to hide how happy she was that she'd pulled out a win, even if she still had so much to learn. "Thank you, kind sir."

He put one leg forward, leaned down so his nose was touching his foot: a horse's bow and she laughed at the courtliness of the move.

"You want an apple, Channel?"

"They're yours."

"I can share."

"It's not really apples I want." He moved closer.

"Oh. I—I can't share more than that. I have someone."

"He's not here. You left him."

"I didn't 'leave him' leave him. I just came over to Europe for a while. We're in a long-distance relationship." It was something Janice had said last time Sapphira had talked to her. And it made sense.

"My mistake." He moved back.

"You sure you don't want an apple? Those I can share." She made her voice as gentle and non-flirting as she could.

"I'll take one then." He leaned in and took the apple closest to them, chewing thoughtfully.

"What?" She quickly ate one, and then two of the other apples. She loved this variety: it wasn't one she'd had before coming here. Leland said they were some kind of heirloom apples, grown only on a few farms. Smaller than what she was used to but so juicy.

"You should aim for the Jockey Club Stakes."

"You think I'm ready for that? It's a Group 2 race, isn't it?"

"I don't think you're ready for it right this moment, but it's not till late April. You'll have ample time to train and get in more preps. I think it's a good goal."

"I'll talk to Leland about it."

"Good." He lowered his head, and she knew he wanted to nuzzle her but was respecting what she'd said. "Congratulations again."

"Thank you." She watched him walk off, then went back to her apples.

One week ran into the next, the time broken up by more races, harder company, Sapphira came in fourth her first time in Group 3 company, done in by the mad rush from the field behind her. Leland lectured her on her tendency to park herself in no man's land. Channel watched a replay of the race and showed her where he thought she went wrong and where he would have chosen to stalk from. Her next race she did better, finishing in the money at least with a close third.

Running clockwise or on long straightaways no longer seemed so foreign. Holding back and staying with the field became easier to do. Stalking meant something different here, and she wanted to prove she was adaptable.

And after each race, she'd call Gray. Usually he'd seen a replay of the race and would have his own comments, but he understood it was different, that even he might have to adapt his preferred style a little bit. Although he liked to stay in the back and then charge at the end, so he'd probably feel right at home here.

When she finally won several Group 3 races, Leland told her to take a break, go back to training, and rest up for the Jockey Club Stakes. Sapphira needed the break and took to running early in the morning when it was very cool and the dew was on the grass. Then she'd do another gallop later in the afternoon, just before sunset.

She was just coming in from her morning run when she saw Leland looking for her. "Gray called. Come on, we'll see if he's still there."

Leland called Janice and then set the phone up in Sapphira's stall, the video chat window showing Gray. He seemed distracted.

"What's going on?"

"I just wanted you to know I finalized the purchase of the land for Dawn Enterprises. I took all the things you've told me about the farm you're at now into consideration."

"That's great. Congratulations." She wanted to nose the phone in some kind of pretend nuzzle but was afraid she'd knock it over or disconnect the video chat session. Being this far away was so unsatisfying. "So did you find out if there's any way you can watch my race live?"

They'd talked about him trying.

He looked down. "I'm going to try, but I've got a race."

"You do? I thought you said you were free that weekend?" She'd harbored hopes he might come over to England but had decided not to broach it when he seemed more and more entrenched in making his farm a reality.

"I was. But now Oaklawn's offered a bonus to the Boundless Iron purse if I run—Joe's already in—and it's not just for win but second too. It'll be a substantial amount of cash, and I'm a little cash poor at the moment."

She had lots of cash. Not dollars but pounds. Worth more than dollars. But Gray had never asked her for any. Maybe that was good. Money would just be a complication between them. Muddy the waters.

"Sapphira? Are you disappointed? I'll catch it on replay. They'll have vids up somewhere."

"Sure. No. That makes sense."

Suddenly she heard a horse behind her, Channel's soft voice saying, "We just got more of those apples you like. I—oh, I'm sorry."

She turned and saw him looking at the phone. "I'm on a call."

"Right. Sorry." And he was gone.

"Who was that? I heard him, but I couldn't really see him."

"Just one of the horses here. We've been out of apples—well, the kind I like and I guess we just got more in. Yay." She was talking too much.

"So…he's a friend."

"He's been really helpful, yeah." She shook her head slightly, something she did when she was nervous. "So tell me about the farm."

It took him a moment; he seemed intent on studying her—or as much as he could through the video chat connection—then he finally began to talk.

The farm sounded beautiful. He was excited. She just wished he'd get as excited about her.

"Are you nervous or something?" Sapphira asked Leland, who was walking back and forth more than her norm and seemed impatient to get the van backed up.

"No, love. Why?"

"You're pacing."

"Oh. Well. Big races today."

Sapphira knew Leland was probably more worried about her chances in the Jockey Club Stakes than about Channel in the 3,000 Guineas, one of the many races created when hybrid horses began to race more often, like the old iron horses of old—before horses started breaking down even though they'd barely raced.

"Why aren't I vanning over with Channel? His race is right before mine."

"Pre-race tradition. He's superstitious. Doesn't like to share a van before a race." Leland motioned for her to get in the van. "Just go, all right?"

None of that sounded like Channel, but Sapphira decided not to argue when her trainer was clearly worrying about something. Once she was settled in the van, she thought she heard Leland say, "Yes, I know. Tell him I'm on my way," but the van pulled out before she could hear anything else.

Just as well. She had a race to think about. One and a half miles over Newmarket's mostly straight course with its undulations and dips. She'd gone a mile and three-quarters, so she wasn't worried about the distance, but the competition was another matter. She'd be one of two fillies taking on males in a field of six. She was most worried about Grey Matter, a horse that was actually used to running two miles. This would seem like nothing to him. And he loved Newmarket.

She'd run against two of the others, losing to Exclamation and beating Joust. Pleasant Feather, the other filly, and Cambridge Lad seemed like they were taking a big leap in class. Sapphira hoped they wouldn't be much of a challenge.

She replayed the races she'd watched with Leland, trying to remember each horse's running style and any weaknesses. The van was pulling in before she was ready, and she got off, joining the crowd of other horses coming in from stables all over England. She wouldn't miss this organized chaos. At least when all the horses were stabled at the track, everyone had a place to be before the race. Here, horses just milled around and tried to keep their head in the game while waiting. She saw another of Leland's vans pull in and Channel got off. He came over and stood next to her, his skin twitching like he was already in the gate.

"Nervous?"

"Ready. There's a difference." His words were cocky, but his tone was very gentle.

"I really like you."

He turned to her, confusion in the set of his head.

"I don't mean like-like. I mean…you're so nice. And I really appreciate that. And I want you to win today." She reached out and nuzzled him in a way that wasn't at all flirtatious. Just friendly. Just supportive.

"I wish you felt more for me."

"I know." She pulled away. "But I've got a stallion waiting for me at home." Or at least residing at home—waiting for her might be stretching it. Working hard on his farm and not even noticing she wasn't there most of the time was probably more like it.

The officials called for the horses for the 3,000 Guineas, and Channel said, "Come over. Watch the race."

"Okay." She looked back at her driver who was on the phone and didn't seem to notice she was leaving. Oh well, he'd figure out where she'd gone.

She followed Channel, and took her place in the observation area at the finish line. Channel weighed in and then trotted down the track, getting smaller and smaller the further away he went down the massive straight of the Rowley Mile course.

Her race would start even further back, on the Beacon course, which served the same purpose as the chutes in American racing, adding the extra distance onto the ten-furlong straight.

She heard the announcer say the horses were ready and had to take his word for it since the gate was so far away, then they were off. As she expected, Channel held off, hanging in the middle of the tightly bunched field for most of the mile race, then exploded as was his way at the end, bursting through with a breathtaking turn of foot.

A lot of people and horses were cheering him on as he flashed by the stands. When he trotted back to be weighed out, he nodded to her and she pawed the ground and dipped her head, letting him know she approved of his effort.

She was called by the officials before the ceremonies for the 3,000 Guineas were over and she weighed in, then trotted down the long course with its dip at the end, using the time to warm up and try to get the markers into her head. There was no last turn to use as a cue for when to make her run. But she'd run this course before and done fine.

She blew hard, did it again, trying to work out the jitters she felt. Pleasant Feather trotted by her, tail up like some kind of Arabian, her chestnut coat gleaming. If there were a prettiest filly award, she'd win hands down, but fortunately this wasn't a beauty contest. Not that Sapphira was a slouch in the looks department.

Grey Matter was ahead of them, and Sapphira glanced back and saw three brown horses trailing behind. She had no idea which was which without seeing the numbers on their weight harness, but knew they were Exclamation, Joust and Cambridge Lad.

She turned left, onto Beacon and saw the gate ahead. She was post three, but it really didn't matter in a race this long. She'd noticed Channel moving from the inside to the middle of the main track— the going must be better there. She didn't know if the others had been paying attention to the race or not: they might not know how the track was running.

One of the brown horses loaded first—Joust, she realized as she saw him go into post four. Then the others followed. She was the last to load, which was fine with her. She got settled and the gates opened.

Grey Matter went to the front and then slowed them down. If

the others realized how slow they were going, they showed no sign of it, so Sapphira decided stalking was out and went after Grey Matter, sitting right off his cheek, and he picked up the pace rather than let her pass.

Didn't like to be headed? Not unlike Joe. She'd never run against him, but she'd thought of what she'd do if she did. And it worked out a lot like this, not letting the stallion pull a fast one on the field by running fractions so slow they might as well be cantering.

But there was a point where she needed to drop back and resume stalking. Once the pace seemed fair to her, she let him go on and settled into the one turn before the massive straightaway.

She was a length clear of the others so she eased out onto the middle of the track and found it much less spongy than the inner portion had been. Grey Matter was still near the rail and Pleasant Feather passed her going after him, also on the inside.

The brown trio stayed behind her, in the center, leading to two distinct groups racing down the course, something that would never happen in American Racing but wasn't uncommon here. The problem with not being directly behind the lead horses was it was hard to judge how far ahead Grey Matter and Pleasant Feather really were.

Sapphira wanted to run after them, but they still had a half mile left to race. Four furlongs that included the two-furlong fall and rise of the Dip at the end. She had to save her energy for the right moment. That was the essence of racing here. Most of the horses she'd raced here made one big move and that was it. If they'd gone after Grey Matter the way she had, many of them probably would have stayed with him and hoped for the best.

But that's why Leland brought her over. Because she wasn't going to do what everyone expected.

She felt the pounding of the three browns getting closer and saw the marker she liked to cut loose at approaching. The two up front were pulling away, so she quickened her stride before she normally would, letting the good ground under her feet help her along, enjoying the feel of racing, giving it her all—which was a good deal better with all the conditioning she'd done.

She was eating up ground and Pleasant Feather was tiring. She passed her and went after Grey Matter, who was still on the rail and seemed content to stay there. She dug deep, forced her stride to quicken just a little more and she began to eat up the distance between her and Grey Matter.

They hit the downslope of the Dip and she thought she was at his shoulder. By the start of the rise, they seemed neck and neck. She could tell he was giving it everything he had, and she still couldn't tell exactly how close she was since he was so far to the right of the course. So she reached for just a little more as she took her last strides up the rise and to the finish line.

They went through together and she had no idea if she'd won or not.

Then she peeked at the big screen that let the spectators see the race and saw her number at the top. She galloped out, heard people cheering, and saw Grey Matter go by her, his expression stormy. The way she imagined Joe might look if she beat him. Or if Gray did, later today.

She turned and as she trotted back down the track, she saw a familiar dappled-gray back in the horse's viewing area, then the horse turned to look at her, his eyes gleaming. Gray?

She slowed and walked over to him. "You're here?"

"I'm here."

"But your race?"

"I decided this was more important. And I'm glad I did. You ran a hell of a race."

She felt a warm rush of pleasure. He'd come all this way? And skipped a very lucrative race? "Thanks." She heard a horse coming up behind her, turned and saw it was Channel. "This is—"

"I'd have to be an idiot not to know who this is. Nice race, earlier. Guess you're afraid to take on my girl here?" Gray sounded way too possessive, but it made Sapphira laugh.

"She's an incredibly talented filly." Channel shot her a look full of regard, then seemed to be waiting for her. "You need a lift?"

"I've got my own van. See you back at the farm," she said, and Channel, with a bit of a sad look, trotted off.

"Handsome horse."

"Mmmm, if you like them young." She wanted to nuzzle Gray: he smelled so good, like home and everything she missed.

"That's the apple guy, right?" He said it with so much sarcasm she laughed.

"Yep. Apple guy."

"Well, if you like Horse of the Year types, I guess he's okay."

He stamped his foot, and she thought it was an unconscious gesture, a little bit of insecurity in the middle of his derision even if he'd been Horse of the Year once, too. "Go on. Weigh out. Get your accolades. I'll be right here when you're done."

She nuzzled him, then trotted off, enjoying the restrained roar of the crowd. Like their counterparts across the pond, these English bettors loved it when a filly beat the boys.

Once she was done with the pomp and presentations, she headed back out to the track. Gray was true to his word, still where he'd said he'd be, but he was talking with some mares about Dawn Enterprises and what he could offer as a sire. As soon as he saw her, he said, "I've got to go," and left them to join her.

"Sure you want to leave them just like that? Not the best way to do business."

"I know but I did it, didn't I? For my best girl."

She arched her neck, feeling good, feeling like she had when they'd first met, when he'd made her feel like she was the only filly in the world for him. "So my van's waiting if you want to see the stables I've been telling you so much about."

"I'd like that. Anna offered me a tour before she brought me to the track, but I told her I'd wait to let you show me around."

"She knew you were coming?" And had kept it as surprise. Her weird behavior before the race suddenly made sense.

"She gave me a ride from the airport." He laughed. "You think I accomplished all this on my own? Needed a little inside help." He nuzzled her and she pressed her head against his. "I've missed you, Sapphira. That other stuff—the farm, whatever mares come my way, the racing—that's business. This…this is the heart, you know?"

She felt a warm glow. He wasn't usually so…gushy. "But you have business while you're here, I'm sure."

"I don't actually."

"You came all this way…just for me?"

He nuzzled her again, murmuring, "I wish you didn't sound so surprised."

"I just…I wasn't sure why you wanted me around."

"I want you around because I'm crazy about you. You're my girl. But—and this is hard for me to say but I'm going to say it, because it needs to be said—who you breed with, well, that's your concern. That's your *business* and I'm not going to stand in the way of that. But where you live—I want you to think of the farm as your home. Give birth there. I'll treat your foals right, whether they're mine or someone else's. Be the first lady of *our* farm."

Our farm. She loved that. "So if I wanted to mate with Channel, you'd be okay with that."

"If you wanted to mate with him because it made financial or career sense, then yes. If you're madly in love with him, then no, I'd have a problem with that."

She laughed and knocked him. "Big goof."

"But your goof." He moved closer and seemed to sigh.

"When did you get in?"

"This morning. I'm exhausted. Now I understand what you meant about jetlag."

"My hero, enduring all this just for me." She got him moving with her, walking slowly back to the vanning area.

"Sapphira, I know you have more races to conquer here and in Ireland and France."

"Maybe Germany, too."

"Okay. There, too. And I can't promise I'll be at them all—I've got races to run I can't scratch out of and there's the farm. But I'll be at the ones I can. Because you matter to me. I love you."

She closed her eyes and let him chew lightly on her neck as they walked. "I love you, too."

"So you're not madly in love with Channel?"

She laughed. "No. Although he'd be way less work."

"Anything worth having is worth working for. That's a lesson I've taken to heart, and I'm sorry if I made you think I didn't care. But you coming over here was the wake-up call I needed. There's business and then there's us."

"I like that there's still an us."

"I'd be very sad if there weren't."

She led him to her van. The driver was leaning against it. "Good race, then?"

"Where have you been? She beat 'em all, buddy." Gray sounded very protective—and very proud.

"Yes, it was a good race." She urged Gray into the van before he could berate the driver any more than he had. "Come on. Come see my home away from home."

"You do know that, as much as I might learn by seeing it, I'm going to compare it unfavorably to the spot I've bought for Dawn Enterprises, right?"

She knocked against him gently, thinking already about their farm, how pretty it would be when she finally did come home. "Wouldn't be you if you didn't."

Rivals and Other Complications

Stellar Song eased off the van that brought him to the track and stood for a moment, taking in the sights and sounds and smells, then he heard a familiar nicker and a voice saying, "Took you long enough to get here."

He turned and saw Copperhead coming up, his bright chestnut coat gleaming in the sunshine. "I was worried you weren't coming," Copperhead said.

"And miss beating your ass in the Invitational? Hardly." Stellar moved closer, nodding to his people as they started to move his stuff into the barn his farm was using, but then walking away from the hubbub with Copperhead, content to catch up and just be with the colt who was his nemesis on the track and his best friend off.

A black filly, big as a colt, kicked up her heels at him as she walked by. "Stellar Song. Be still my heart."

"Daffodil." He turned back to Copperhead, muttered, "Fillies," and his friend laughed.

"So I heard Runaway Joe made you an offer to stand at his farm." As always, Copperhead danced a little as he walked, like he was full of pent-up energy he didn't know what to do with.

"Yeah. He wants a turf sire. He's never taken to that surface."

"You going to do it?"

Stellar thought about the big stallion's offer, how charming he had been as he'd made the case for why Stellar Song was the perfect complement to him in terms of what mares would look for. He knew Runaway Joe was just thinking of his bottom line, though. This had nothing to do with any true regard for Stellar. "I don't think so."

"It's a good offer. Or that's what I heard."

"It's a great offer. But...I'm not quite ready to get into the stud thing, you know?" He studied Copperhead. "You've had offers, too, from what I've heard. What's your excuse?"

Copperhead danced some more, kicking up dust on the path. "Settle on some boring farm and watch other horses take my glory? No thanks."

"But eventually…?"

"Is that what you want to do? Retire? What happened to us going to France and Ireland? To Japan and Australia? I mean sure we've done here and Canada and a few races in England, but there are still battlefields to conquer. And its way more fun doing that with you."

"I know," Stellar said. "But those offers…I mean look at Gray Dawn. You get a few off races and people lose interest."

"He had more than a few off races."

"Right but still—"

"Then we do like Gray's doing and open a farm of our own. Only we'll be honest when we name it: Loser's Alley or Washed-Up Run."

Stellar laughed because Copperhead probably wasn't kidding. He'd name it that, and people would love it, and between them, they'd have amazing foals and make a ton of money. "And before that, we race anywhere we want to? Like we used to say we would when we were newbies?"

"Exactly."

He heard his manager Louisa calling for him. "I've gotta go. I'll come find you later."

"I'm in barn seven."

"Okay." Stellar turned and headed back to his barn, but at the last minute glanced back. Copperhead was standing on the path, watching him, then he flicked his tail and turned, hurrying off.

Stellar watched him for a moment, then turned away laughing. Washed-Up Run really would be a hilarious name for a farm.

Stellar poked the straw around his stall until he had it just the way he liked it.

Louisa relaxed in the folding lounge chair she brought wherever they went. "We've got to talk about the offer from Runaway Farms." She sighed, as if she found managing a top turf horse challenging. "It's an incredible offer. And Joe is super picky. Horses have been wooing *him* trying to get on his farm."

"I know."

"So…? What's the problem?"

"I'm just not ready, okay?"

"You're five years old, Stell. Most horses have spawned a foal or two by that age. People are starting to talk."

"Talk? About what?"

"That maybe you're infertile. That's why you aren't taking any offers."

He kicked the straw around the ground. "That's stupid. I'm just not ready for that life."

"Are you ever going to be? I've seen how the fillies flirt with you. I've also seen how you don't flirt back."

"Since when is flirting a requirement? I'm a racer and I've got my mind on business. I win. A lot of the time—and you get to enjoy a cut of that so I fail to see the problem." His voice was rising, and he was kicking the ground hard enough to raise dust.

"Fine. I'm just—" Her attention seemed to be caught by something just behind him. "Of course. He's here."

Stellar turned and saw Copperhead walking toward them, and felt an instant surge of relief. "Hey."

"Hey. Am I interrupting something?"

"Yes," Louisa said at the same time he said, "No."

"You two need to get your story straight."

"We're in the middle of something."

"No," Stellar said, "we're really not. We're done talking about it right now."

She rolled her eyes.

Copperhead shot him a commiserating glance; he often said two-leggers were necessary but a complete pain in the ass, and today Stellar couldn't disagree. "You want to check out the track? They re-seeded it for this meet. The grass is amazing I've been told. Today's the first day they're letting us on it."

"Sure." Stellar looked at Louisa. "You have objections?"

"Nope." She picked up a magazine and made a big show of not being interested in him.

"What's her problem? Other than being a two-legger?" Copperhead asked once they were out of earshot.

"She really wants me to take the offer from Runaway Farms."

"Yeah because she's no doubt writing herself a big cut of the deal—are you paying attention to the fine print?"

Stellar sighed. "She's my friend. I shouldn't have to."

"There are no two-legged friends in business."

"Joe has them. Gray Dawn does too."

"The exceptions that prove the rule."

"Anyway, she's annoyed because I won't just do what she says." Like he had for so long if he was honest, since he'd paid his way off his home farm and she'd taken him on after his first race, urging him to move off dirt and onto grass even though his pedigree screamed dirt horse. "I mean she's gotten me where I am so I have no complaints, but this decision I'm entitled to make on my own."

"On that we can agree." Copperhead dipped his head, biting at Stellar playfully. "So you really think you can beat me on Sunday."

"I've done it plenty of times." And been beaten by Copperhead plenty of times. After they'd gotten through a bumpy early two-year-old season—one that had been memorable more for meeting each other than how fast they were progressing on the track—they'd taken turns winning most of the big grass races. They'd missed out on two-year-old honors, but Stellar had been champion turf horse two years ago, and Copperhead had won the voting last year.

Copperhead tried to bite him again, and Stellar bumped him, the way he used to play with the other yearlings in the pastures where he'd grown up. Most horses lost the ability to play when they were at their level—business face and all that. But Stellar thought he and Copperhead were still so fresh because of the fun they got up to, not in spite of it. He wasn't sure what he'd do without him.

"Come on, slowpoke," Copperhead said as he set off onto the track at a fast trot.

Stellar caught him easily and they worked their way over to the entrance to the grass, leaving the dirt for the surface they both pre-ferred. "Wow, this is nice."

"Right?" Copperhead shook his head as one of the officials at the gap told them not to gallop, just to walk. "What fun is that?"

"If it can't take a few horses warming up, it won't hold up to races." Stellar laughed softly. "Since when do we not gallop on grass? I mean what are they going to do to us? We're the main draw for this weekend."

"Damned straight. Race you?"

"You got it."

They took off together, and Stellar heard the official yell some-thing at them but they were gone too fast to make out the words.

He didn't care anyway, not when he was finally running the way he liked to, he and Copperhead in perfect rhythm, his friend's chestnut legs hitting down, Stellar like a bay shadow, two horses with one stride.

They hit the turn and saw the official waving his arms, standing in their way. Slowing, they moved away from the rail and Copperhead threw his head up as they passed the two-legger.

"Damn it, you two," was all Stellar heard and then they were galloping again, and he gave himself over to what he loved.

Running. And his best friend.

They came around the turn and slowed to a walk, moving to the far outside of the track.

"Nice job with the re-seeding," Copperhead said to the official. "We were happy to test it out for you."

"Smart ass," the guy muttered, and Stellar laughed because Copperhead was exactly that.

Stellar tended to be serious, thinking things over so hard and long he missed out on the fun of life sometimes. He never felt like he was missing out when Copperhead was around.

They went through the gap and onto the main track.

"I'm not ready to go back," Stellar murmured.

"I'm not either. Let's show these dirt nags how it's done."

Stellar laughed and then let himself be in the moment, running in tandem on the dirt, passing other horses, being passed by others as they got tired. Not worrying.

This was how life should always be.

Sunday came quickly, the time between his arrival and the race lost in a haze of gallops with Copperhead and strategy sessions with Louisa and Mister Moss, an old crank of a horse who consulted when he felt like it. He'd been a hellion on the track back in the day, winning two Horse of the Year awards in a row. He'd been training other horses for nearly two decades. Mating when he felt like it, passing on his genes, but never settling down at any one farm. The only things he seemed committed to were being a cantankerous old S.O.B. who could say whatever he wanted and his cat, Lulu.

But he brought insight into the horses Stellar would be facing in Sunday's race, a kind of bone-deep understanding Stellar hadn't seen replicated in any other horse or two-legger. So he put up with Moss's attitude and his nasty-tempered feline since it meant getting an edge on the competition.

Now he watched as that competition walked onto the dirt track, having their weights checked, and then warming up. Copperhead found him and they jogged around the track together, waiting for the officials to open up the gap to the grass.

"You work with Mister Moss and the cat from hell?" Copperhead asked as they hit the backstretch.

Stellar laughed. "Yep. You?"

"Yeah. There are so many shippers from overseas running today, and nobody knows the international players like he does."

"I know. But man, the price of doing business."

Copperhead laughed. "Tell me about it. And that damn cat. Did she jump on your back? I swear she knows I hate that."

She had not jumped on Stellar's back, but he was probably better at treating her like she was some kind of royalty than Copperhead was.

The gap was open, so they trotted through and headed for the starting gate.

"See you at the finish line," Copperhead said as he headed for his post on the rail.

Stellar was in an outside post and thought he'd gotten the better deal, although both he and Copperhead liked to hang back, so the break wasn't that important to either of them. Most of the European shippers would break slow and run covered up, happy to stay behind the frontrunners until it was time to break out and have one mad dash at the end. There was a Japanese horse who liked to take the lead and try to run off with the race. Stellar was hoping one of the local boys who also liked to be in front would keep him in check.

The gates closed and he got on his toes. He might not want to dash out like some jackrabbit, but he also didn't want to get caught flat footed. The doors slammed open and he was away. As he slipped over toward the inside, getting settled in behind a wall of the rest of the horses, he saw Copperhead boxed in at the rail, nearly running up on the heels of one of the Europeans to the point where he seemed about to go down, but then he recovered.

But then he began to lose ground, the other horses moving

away, and Stellar was about to pass him when he saw Copperhead take another bad step, lurch toward the rail, then try to recover, bearing out.

Stellar could have kicked away and been clear but instead he moved closer, bumping hard against Copperhead and keeping him upright as he slowed.

"What are you doing?" Copperhead was looking at him like he was crazy.

"Are you okay?"

"I'll be fine. Go win this thing."

Stellar saw the field ridiculously far ahead of him. Then he heard Copperhead say, "You can do it. I know you can. Run!"

So he ran. Faster and harder than he'd ever run before. He caught up with the stragglers by the first turn, spent the whole of the backstretch getting into some kind of position near the main pack. He felt winded, wasn't sure he had more in him, but as they hit the far turn, he saw Copperhead standing up ahead in the observation area, a medic working on his leg.

"Go, damn it! If I'm out, you need to pay for our airfare to France!" Copperhead was laughing as he yelled at him.

France now. Not later. New rules and faces and historic races they could run in. He didn't have to leave Copperhead behind; he didn't have to go to Joe's and follow his rules. And he didn't have to stop racing—stop having fun with his best friend by his side.

He found something deep within himself, some new gear and he used it, flying down the track, knowing that if Copperhead hadn't been hurt, he'd be right there, matching him stride for stride.

He caught the now tiring frontrunners halfway down the homestretch, set his sights on the horse in the lead, one of the Europeans. He ground down the last few strides, coming closer and closer and then…there.

But was it enough?

He looked up at the board as they galloped out. The "Photo" sign was flashing. So was the "Inquiry" sign, but that was standard whenever a horse was hurt. Stellar didn't think the stewards would ding the European for his actions—Copperhead had been too eager, shouldn't have run up on him that way. But he raced like he lived life: all in.

As Stellar trotted back, he heard a disappointed roar from the crowd. He knew without looking the other horse had nosed him out of the win, leaving a lot of bettors disappointed.

He ignored the crowd and the officials who wanted to weigh him out and made his way to Copperhead. "Are you all right?"

"They don't think it's broken. But it looks like I'll be out for a bit."

"Well, France is a nice place to recuperate, right?" Stellar moved closer and saw Copperhead's expression change, his body language go from cocky to something softer—Stellar so rarely saw him let down this way, showing his heart in a world that could be harsh.

He nuzzled Copperhead gently on the neck and felt him return the affection. They stood there, necks pressed together, then Stellar murmured, "And while you recuperate, I'll get a head start on making a name for the terrible American twosome."

"I won't be out for long. Just need some pasture rest."

"Good, then after we tear up France, we can come back here for the Turf Cup at the end of the year to see which of us is champion this year."

"It'll be me."

Their old game, continuous one-upmanship. Stellar loved hearing it because it meant Copperhead wasn't lying about the severity of his injury. He heard the official calling him and yelled, "In a minute," then turned back to Copperhead. "So, France, okay? Together?"

Copperhead nosed him. "Yeah, France. Now, go let them weigh you out before they disqualify you for colluding."

Stellar laughed and with a last nuzzle, trotted off to the officials.

Colluding with his best friend. That sounded pretty sweet—and really, really fun.

Mister Moss and His Cat

"You ready, Lulu?" Mister Moss asked, as he climbed into the luxury horse van that carted him around from track to track.

The black cat took a last look around—probably checking to make sure there weren't any mice or birds handy for a quick pre-trip snack—and then jumped into the van with him. Roscoe closed the doors and got into the driver's seat, looking back and saying, "You all good back there?" before starting the van up and pulling out.

"Why the hell did we come to this backwater?" Moss muttered as he lay down in the very cushy straw. It was his favorite kind of bedding, expensive and hard to get. He'd earned a ton of money when he was racing, and he charged exorbitant rates to consult so his bottom line was still excellent. He could afford whatever he wanted.

Except some things couldn't be bought, like hope when he was on a back-of-beyond track like the one they were leaving. He'd watched horse after horse, anticipating finding a diamond in the rough—he also acted as talent scout for several farms—but all he'd seen were lumps of coal. Horses finishing out of the money for the umpteenth time, losing to horses just starting out and looking for easy wins. Losing to horses that would move on and probably never see these tracks again, while the losers would be lucky if they could afford to stay.

They'd go back to the farms they were born at and try to work off their foaling fee but probably never pay it off completely. They'd die still encumbered. Still owned.

Some of them were emotionally broken. Coming to him, begging him for help, for any little nugget he could give. He used to try to help them all, but now he'd had time to see that no matter what he did, it usually didn't help the horses who were stuck.

But every now and then he saw a horse who was at rock bottom but still had some fight left in him. Was a bit of a jerk, maybe. Not ready to admit he was a loser. Moss liked those horses. He usually tried to hook them up with a horse or a two-legger that might be able to offer them a new life. He'd done that at their last stop for a liver chestnut with a bad attitude that rivaled Lulu on a good day. Had pointed him out to a shrink who'd approached Moss about getting a hybrid horse to work at her therapy ranch. Red Scorpion had been his name—a good name, Moss thought. Matched his "screw you" attitude.

The doc had looked at him like he was crazy. But Moss could tell about horses and two-leggers, could see what made them tick. And she'd seemed to trust that. Moss had a reputation, after all.

Lulu walked over and kneaded him until he moved over; he'd known he was lying in her favorite spot and she didn't much care that every nice thing in her life came courtesy of Moss's money. Cats were famous for doing their own thing, but Lulu took it to a whole new level, never doing what anyone said. Unless food was involved.

He respected her priorities.

She stretched out with her paws on his back, and soon was making the sounds he associated with Roscoe when he slept—the grunts and snorts of an old two-legger. It was the last thing you'd expect from a cat who tolerated very little in the way of disrespect —that she'd make such unabashed sounds of pleasure or regret or whatever else she was feeling as she dreamed.

It was probably why Moss loved her. He loved so little anymore.

"You still want to go to Oklahoma, boss?" Roscoe's voice was always so damn cheerful.

"I'm sick of the southwest. Let's go somewhere else."

"Fine by me? Florida? New York? Kentucky? California? Hell, you want to take a run up to Canada? Our papers are all in order." Roscoe sounded like any one of those places would make him happy. Moss wondered what it was about driving a cantankerous old horse and a bitchy cat around that made Roscoe so relentlessly upbeat.

But it also made him nice to have around. Moss never had to worry about offending him. "Just pick one and let me know when we're there."

"You got it." Roscoe did something on the van's GPS and then after a bit of turns and stops, Moss could tell they'd hit the inter-state. Wherever they were headed was fine.

He woke up hours later, Lulu stretched across his front legs, pinning him down the way she liked to do. "Move it," he said as gruffly as he could, but the fact he was careful not to move his legs probably made him sound less dominant than he wanted. "Lulu, damn it all, get up."

She opened her eyes a slit, rolled off him, and stretched out in the straw. Leaving it to him to get up without stepping on her.

A power play. And one he fell for every time he damn near did injury to himself trying to get up without disturbing her.

He could hear her purring as he went to his water bucket. He was sure she could understand two-leggers and horses, but she had never once spoken back. It was probably beneath her dignity.

He walked over and nosed her, earning an offended "mroowt" and a swipe at his face. He just laughed and moved over to the opening that let him talk to Roscoe. "So where we headed?"

"California, here we come. Right back where we started from." Roscoe was singing, which didn't bug Moss much since he had a pleasant voice. "I called ahead. Reserved you a stall. I told them a week. You think you're going to stay longer?"

"Dunno. Usually good picking there. I may."

"Well they said just to let them know. Santa Anita's always so accommodating to you."

"I won a shitload of races there."

"No cause to swear."

"My van, my rules." It was an old argument. One Moss won because he could fire Roscoe whenever he wanted the way he'd fired the two-leggers who'd preceded him. But Moss thought Lulu would be very upset with him. She loved the way Roscoe brushed her, and he was always slipping her treats.

What Moss did for this damn cat.

The damn cat chose that moment to jump to his back, sitting easily as he swayed with the motion of the van. He didn't allow her to do this when they were around other horses or any two-leggers other than Roscoe. Had bucked her off the times she tried. But when they were alone, he allowed it.

Besides, it felt good the way she kneaded his back.

"Someone called for you while you were asleep."

"Imagine that." His voicemail was always full. Everyone wanted his help with something.

"It was Joe."

"Really? I thought he was boycotting my services since that last argument we had."

"So did I. But he said it's important. You want me to dial him?"

"Yeah, I guess." He'd been a mentor to Joe and had watched him grow up from a precocious two-year-old to being one of the best horses running. But that didn't mean they got along all the time. The more famous Joe got the less he liked hearing the truth from Moss. Moss took exception to that and sugar-coated his words even less. Trouble ensued.

It was how things were.

Roscoe pulled off at a rest stop, dialed the number for Joe and once he talked to Joe's two-legger Haley, put the phone up where Moss could hear and talk.

"Moss?" Joe sounded as imperious as ever.

"No, it's some other equine consultant."

"Funny. Look, I need a favor."

"Last I checked, son, we weren't talking."

"I'm not your damn son. And we're still not talking. But…this is different. This is family. I have a colt running at Santa Anita. I know you're headed there because Roscoe told Haley you were."

Moss was going to have to talk to Roscoe again about discretion and whose business it was where they went. "Which of your sons and why?"

"Comet Trail, and I think he's doping. He's been running phenomenally, but I've heard things I don't like about his behavior."

"The track officials run random checks for drugs."

"And you and I both know that for the right amount of money you can get designer-made crap so new the tests don't check for the ingredients. Just, look him over. I trust you. If you tell me he's winning all on his own, I'll listen."

And the hell of it was, Joe probably would. Moss could lecture him all day about finding a new strategy for winning and get nowhere, but when it came to his family, Joe would be all ears. "All right. How's Flicker doing?"

He laughed as he heard Joe start breathing hard. The stallion couldn't stand that colt, and Moss wasn't sure if it was because he was winning everything he tried his hand at—the Derby being the most recent thing—or if it was because he had Joe's favorite daughter completely enamored. "Gonna let you go now, Joe. You take care."

He pushed the phone into Roscoe's lap, who hung up on Joe before Joe could say anything smart back. That was another reason to keep Roscoe around. He was well trained.

"I'm going to stretch my legs, take a little personal break. You want out?" Roscoe was already opening his door.

"Yes. But don't let Lulu out."

"I know the drill, boss. Nothing's going to happen to your cat."

Lulu, as always, seemed to know exactly what was up and made for the van door as soon as she heard the electric ramp being engaged.

"No you don't, Lulu," Moss said, as he began the ridiculous dance of trying to stop a determined cat from doing what she wanted.

And failed. Fortunately, Roscoe was ready for her as he opened the door a tiny bit, grabbed her by the scruff, and held her, somehow managing not to get scratched as Moss came out. Then he eased the door nearly shut, pushed her through the opening, and closed it before she could try again.

Moss observed the process carefully. Damn cat had nearly played in traffic the last time she'd gotten out at a rest stop. Smart she might be, but there were times he thought she lost all sense of self-preservation at the idea of a little fun.

"Your kitty is fine, boss. I won't be long."

"I will be so take your time."

Roscoe laughed and waved in a way that could mean anything. It was the safest answer he could probably give.

Moss studied Joe's boy as the colt warmed up on the track for the featured race. Comet Trail looked good, nearly as black as his father, not quite as big—his mother, Trailing Comet, had been a little thing. The colt had definitely named himself after her: no love lost for his father. As far as Moss knew, Runaway Comet wasn't taken yet. But this colt hadn't asked him for naming advice, or any advice, really.

Moss missed the familiar feeling of Lulu rubbing against his legs. The track officials had banned her from the front-side after she attacked a filly who'd kicked her during a consultation. She hadn't kicked hard, but enough to piss the cat off beyond measure —something Moss had told the filly would come back to haunt her. He just hadn't expected Lulu to attack her on the way to the winner's circle.

He'd actually been tempted to play, "What cat? Not my cat," but everyone knew she was his. So, now, she stayed back with Roscoe in the barns. Sometimes locked in his stall if she looked like she was determined to wander trackside.

Comet Trail turned and trotted by Moss again, his hide shining brightly, slipping easily over muscles that didn't seem out of line for what Moss would expect for a colt his age and size. He'd like to tell Joe he was crazy, but Moss had taken a turn around the barns and seen which two-leggers Comet Trail was talking to in the shedrow, and they were not what Moss would call clean. They'd been cited before for doping offenses, and horses working with them had been suspended—in one case for life when the mare in question had multiple offenses.

Not good. Moss hated to see a horse being manipulated by two-leggers. Then again, Comet Trail didn't look like he was one to do anything he didn't want to do. In that, he was just like his father.

The horses were out of sight on the backstretch, heading to the chute where the gate for the start of this six-furlong sprint was set up. Comet Trail was the favorite, followed closely by another front-running colt named Grapple who was getting a lot of attention at the windows. Moss never bet—he made enough money to afford to wager if he wanted to, but he hated throwing money away, and horse racing was nothing if unpredictable, even for a horse who knew the runners as well as he did. Horses had good days and bad days, track surfaces might or might not be to their liking, they might miss the break, get stuck behind horses when they preferred being clear—anything could go wrong.

Moss saw a couple juveniles in the viewing area looking at him, their heads close together as they talked. He was famous, and he didn't take just anyone on as a client. They were probably talking about the best way to approach him. During a race was not it, and he hoped they knew better than to bug him right before a race started.

They seemed to figure that out, staying where they were as the announcer said, "All set. Gates closed. And…they're off."

Moss watched on the big-screen near the tote board, Comet Trail caught a flyer out of the gate and took the lead easily over Grapple, who was caught in traffic. They were flying down the backstretch, the first quarter fractions fast but not suicidal. Comet Trail seemed to catch a breather just before the first turn as Grapple, finally clear, began to make his move away from the rest of the field.

Grapple was at his hip by the middle of the turn, but then Comet Trail dug in, his strides lengthening, his ears pinned back, and Grapple made no more progress. The two colts battled down the stretch this way, both of them clearly giving it their all, but then Grapple started to inch up on Comet Trail. They flashed under the wire, Comet Trail the winner by a shortening head.

Neither he nor Grapple seemed to be joking around as they galloped out. Both looked like they'd given it their best effort and were tired—and the fraction for the last quarter bore that effort out. If Moss had to judge, Comet Trail had won on guts and talent alone, not because of performance-enhancing drugs.

He studied the colt as he trotted to the winner's circle; nothing about him seemed out of sorts. Moss was surprised to see another two-legger walk out to talk to him. A conditioner Moss had worked with—scrupulous with an excellent record. The two other men came over, but the conditioner looked at them the way Moss had looked at the people who'd bankrolled some of his early races when he'd just earned his way away from the farm where he'd foaled. As necessary but unpleasant ways of doing business. If the colt was smart, he'd signed a limited partnership and would ditch them as soon as possible.

Moss didn't plan to ask him. Delving into his financials was way more than he'd told Joe he'd do. He'd tell him his son appeared to be winning on his own but had some unsavory connections. If Joe wanted to do something about that, that was up to him.

Moss turned and eyed the two-year-olds who had been watching him. They both looked uncomfortable. He ambled over, nodding. "You two racing today?"

"No, sir. Just watching to learn."

He liked that. "You raced yet?"

They were both chestnuts but the taller of the two said, "I have. Twice. Haven't broken my maiden yet, came in third last time out."

The other one shook his head. Moss couldn't tell if he just hadn't found the right race or if he was afraid to race—afraid to find out he might not be good at all.

He wasn't sure why, but he felt sorry for them and figured he could help them out, watch a few replays, give advice. Every now and then he felt like doing a good deed. It was rare, but it happened. "I'm staying at barn four. Come see me tonight after the races if you feel so inclined."

They both stammered and said they'd be there. Moss was about to leave when he saw a black shape streaking across the infield on the big screen.

Shit. Lulu.

At least she'd timed it for between races. He was already headed for the official's booth when he heard, "Mister Moss, Mister Moss to the finish line."

Lulu got there before him. She had the officials cornered. Moss nudged her away and shook his head at them. "She's a domestic shorthair. Not a panther."

"Just get her off the track."

"Fine. Fine." He took a deep breath and told her to come. She sat where she was, giving him the look cats had perfected over time. The "I think you may be speaking, but I hear nothing" look. Finally, with a huge sigh, he moved closer so she could jump up on his back. It annoyed the shit out of him that he was having to give her a ride, but it seemed to be the only way.

This was no doubt payback for locking her in the stall.

The crowd laughed and cheered as he trotted off, Lulu riding easily, primarily because she had her claws dug into him in a way that wasn't pleasant.

He cursed her out the entire way to the backside. Roscoe was standing at the fence, his face screwed up in an "I have no idea how this happened" look.

"Get her inside, now. Lock her in the damn van if you have to."

"Boss, it's too warm out to leave her in a car."

"Then put her in a harness. I don't care. Just keep her off the damn track. How am I supposed to scout if you can't do your job?"

"I'm not putting her in a harness, boss." Roscoe grabbed Lulu, who resisted, no doubt leaving claw marks in Moss's fur as she was pulled off—it hurt enough to be bleeding.

She hissed at Moss.

"Yeah, toots, right back at you." He trotted back to the viewing area, hoping Roscoe would keep her under control this time. "Am I bleeding?" he asked the two-year-olds.

"Little bit, yeah," the taller one said.

Damn cat.

When Moss got back to his stall from the viewer enclosure, he heard Lulu long before he saw her, and got a lot of irritated glares from the horses and people in the vicinity.

He let her out, dodging the swipe of her paws as she ran past. Now that the races were over and he was back, she'd stick close to him unless she went hunting. But no one would care what she did, so long as the races weren't underway.

He saw Roscoe had set up his oats the way he liked them, and went in to eat, stopping once to shoo Lulu from sitting on his back. Then he decided to take a walk around the barns, nodding hello as he went, Lulu trotting along beside him with the ineffable grace of a cat.

Suddenly, he saw a familiar sight. Gray Dawn, his dapple-gray coat shining like crazy, standing out in the sun with Deirdre, the blonde girl who seemed to go everywhere with her.

Lulu saw the girl, then Deirdre saw Lulu, and it was like some kind of sappy romance movie as they rushed across the sawdust to get to each other. Lulu leapt into her arms, obviously being far more careful with her claws than normal, and Deirdre somehow got her lying like a baby and was carrying her around murmuring nonsense things to her.

And the damn cat let her do it. In fact, Moss thought he could hear her purring.

He turned away from the undignified spectacle his cat was making of herself, facing Gray Dawn. "Long time, old friend."

Gray glanced at him, then nodded his head up and down—amusement no doubt over what was happening with Lulu. "Very long time. I caught the circus act earlier, her riding you like an old-time bareback rider."

"Very funny. Damn cat gets me into more trouble." He studied

Gray. He knew who was racing the rest of the week and Gray wasn't unless he was a super late entry. Neither was the filly Gray seemed head over heels with—she was tearing up the tracks in Europe. "What are you doing here?"

"Marketing. My farm will be up and running in a few months. Need to get some mares interested in my services."

"Win some more races and you won't have to hard-sell them."

"I have won, you crusty old S.O.B. And you know that because you know everything." Gray danced a little as they stood, clearly full of nervous energy. "Marketing is a good thing."

Moss thought he saw something in Gray's face. "And it takes your mind off missing your filly? I heard varying tales. You got tired of her. She got tired of you. Or that she's just doing what makes the most financial and career sense."

"Nobody got tired of anybody. Sapphira and I are fine." Gray seemed to perk up. "In fact, I've been to Europe several times to see her run. Racking up frequent flyer points like you would not believe."

"Well, good. Nothing like an old fool in love."

"You're just jealous." Gray's words were a bit unkind, but his tone wasn't. He knew more about Moss's story than a lot of others. "When was the last time you had some fun?"

"You mean sired some new spawn? Last year. Pretty little gray made a good case for mating with me."

"Which pretty little gray?"

"Desdemona." Moss laughed. The pretty little gray who was champion older mare the year before and was looking to retire.

Gray knocked him gently with his head in a way Moss normally didn't allow. "But none of them are Trance."

Moss took a deep breath. Not wanting to think about the accident on the road that had killed everyone riding in the van she'd chartered. It had been icy and the driver careless: they'd careened off the road and down an embankment.

The vet had told Moss that Trance hadn't suffered. To this day, he wasn't sure if the man was just being kind or if it was true.

"I don't like to think of her," he finally said, not wanting to examine how his life had changed that day—how his personality had changed. No mare he'd been with had ever come close to what he'd had with Trance.

"Sure. No problem. Let's talk business. I was hoping to catch up with you eventually. Good luck for us you were here on our first stop in the great marketing tour. Deirdre wanted—oh hell, girl, come here and ask him what you want to ask him."

She bounded over, Lulu on her heels, rubbing against her legs as soon as she stopped. "So, Gray says there is no one better at what you do. And...well, my mom is ticked off that I don't want to go to college: I want to help Gray run his farm. And part of that will be training and spotting talent—all the things you do."

Moss waited for her to get to the point of where he helped her.

"I want to...apprentice with you for a while. If you'll have me?"

Lulu set up a rather raucous meowing.

"You don't get a vote," Moss told her. And neither would Roscoe, who would probably love to have another two-legger to hang out with—especially one he'd no doubt adopt as an honorary daughter.

"I don't take on apprentices."

"And I don't leave Gray. So there's a first time for everything." She stood with her arms crossed, looking much older than her years.

"I swear a lot."

"Perfect, so do I. And you won't have some stupid jar I have to put money into every time I do it, right?"

He couldn't help himself; he laughed. "I sure won't. But don't you go to school or something?"

The girl shook her head. "Schools out for summer, but I have to be done by the time it starts back up. Just after Travers Stakes weekend is when my mom said I had to be home."

That might work out well for him. She could keep Lulu off the track during the height of the season, if nothing else. "Her mother's okay with her working for me?" He was looking at Gray, who nodded. Then he turned to Deirdre. "I'm not nice, kid."

"I work with this one," Deirdre said, laughing as she pointed to Gray, "and Lulu—recently voted most evil cat in the world at Churchill—loves me. How much trouble can you be?"

Moss found himself liking this sprite of a girl. "Fine, but we start tonight. Your hours will cease to be your own." He looked at Gray. "That means she's no longer working for you, got it?"

"Yep." Gray and Deirdre said together.

"Fine, two juveniles are stopping by to discuss racing. Deirdre, I'll expect you to pay attention and keep your opinions to yourself until I ask you for them. And the likelihood of me asking for them is slim to none—and slim just left town."

She laughed but then tried to be serious as she said, "Yes, sir."

Gray looked away, clearly amused. Moss had a feeling this girl didn't call anyone "sir."

"So it's settled?" Gray asked, and the look he turned on the girl was full of fondness, possibly the same look Moss often wore when he looked at his blasted cat.

"Yes, damn it all, it's settled. Come on, then."

Gray nodded his thanks, then moved to Deirdre and said something Moss couldn't hear, but the girl threw her arms around Gray's neck and stood there for a long moment before letting him go. He headed back to wherever his stall was, and Deirdre picked up Lulu, holding her close to her face and kissing her on the forehead—did his cat have no dignity?

As he turned, he could have sworn he heard a new voice say, "See, I told you he'd be a pushover."

He swung around. Bringing Deirdre up short. She had a look of "What the hell?" on her face. Lulu had her normal, "You are of limited utility to me, but I'll live with you anyway" expression.

"Did she just say something?"

"She?" Deirdre looked around, then seemed to realize he was staring at the cat "Ohhh, Lulu? No."

As he turned around, he heard, "Everyone knows cats can't talk."

And it wasn't Deirdre's voice saying it.

Damn cat.

What's In a Name?

Everything was dark and warm, the foal was floating and the constant thump-thump of his vessel comforted him, sending him to sleep, easing him when he kicked. Time passed, and he grew, and soon he was eager to shift, to walk, to...run. He tried to move his legs faster but was hindered by the walls of the space that contained him.

Then, one day, everything changed. His vessel was no longer still and comforting but pushing him out, contracting rhythmically, forcing him to move, front legs stretched in front of him, head tucked in, the water he'd floated in so happily gushing around him.

And then he was out, his hooves first, then shins, his nose and face following, a caul over him, making it hard to breathe, when before he'd never thought about it. Water in his mouth, water in his nose, then...air?

Something grabbed his feet, something else was pushing the covering off him, and then another contraction and he was being pulled by whoever had his feet. He moved out more and more and then plopped onto ground soft and giving, but harder than the water had been. And cold.

Sounds. He'd heard things before, but they'd been muffled, but now he heard so clearly. One voice in particular, saying, "Clean his nose out, get the water out."

"Not my first rodeo, Joe." A soft voice, gentle hands, the one who was pulling the caul off held his head so water ran out of his mouth. He rubbed his nose, tickling.

"Colt or filly?" The first voice. A little scary.

"Hold your damn horses, Joe."

"Haley, how hard is it to look?" Then the voice seemed to be directed at something else. "You know, you could rouse yourself to look at our foal."

"I signed up to bear this thing. I did not sign up to mother him."

The foal didn't like the new voice. He knew it was from the thing that had thrown him into this place, and somehow he thought he should want to be near her—that she should want to be near him.

But she moved away rather than closer. He shivered violently, and suddenly there was a new, gentle voice and a golden muzzle thrust against him.

"Let a professional handle this." A tongue lapped against him, and he saw just beyond her golden coat, a small version of her, but dark. "You're going to have to share me with your new brother, Sis," the golden one told the little one, and then she turned to the one who pushed him out. "You can go. They've got a stall ready for you, and Francine will take care of the afterbirth."

The thing that birthed him pushed herself to her feet with a groan and didn't look at him.

He felt...sad. He felt like he should follow her.

Why wouldn't she look at him?

"There, there. Trust me when I say she wouldn't have made much of a mom." It was the gentle voice, the soft hands, and he looked and saw it was someone who stood on two-legs not four. "I'm Haley, and this is Goldie and her little one—your sister now—hasn't picked a name yet, but we call her Sis."

Suddenly the impatient voice was back, saying, "Let me see him."

The space seemed much smaller, blackness taking up the foal's field of vision, but then a nose pushed against his, the soft whuff-whuff taking his scent and giving him his back, and the foal relaxed and met the black one's eyes.

"This is your dad, kiddo." Haley's voice sounded amused and tender, and the foal trusted the dark horse more because the nice two-legger seemed to like him. "Name's Joe. And he's a pain in the ass."

"Language, Haley." Then Joe was pushing against the foal, murmuring, "Help him up."

"He'll get up when he's ready," Goldie said, trying to step between the foal and Joe, but Joe pushed her back gently.

"My kids are precocious."

"Yeah, never let it be said you don't load them up with expectations from day one." Haley was rubbing the foal down and moving his front legs out, in a way that made it easier to try to stand.

The foal pushed, too hard and fell back hard on the ground. Again, and again, and then...up.

"That's my boy."

He was this big horse's boy. But what about the one who had carried him inside her? He tried to look around Joe and Goldie and Sis and see where she'd gone. "Why didn't she want me?" He was shaking on his feet, but he met Joe's eyes. "Why did she leave?"

"Because she's not very nice." Joe eased him from one side toward Goldie, Haley helping him from the other. "Goldie, on the other hand, is the sweetest mare here."

"You say that to all your girls," she said, but she whuffed at him, nose to nose, before turning to help the foal nuzzle under her, until he found her milk.

Heaven. He was in heaven.

"How long do I have to share with him?" he heard the little one—his sister? —ask.

"Forever. Until you don't need milk anymore."

"I don't want to share. Have him find another mother."

Joe laughed and nuzzled her. "Chip off the old block, Sis."

The foal stopped nursing, full and suddenly so tired he could barely stand. Haley held him, helping him step carefully across the hall to a new stall that didn't smell like his not-mother and birth stuff, but like Goldie and Sis.

"Sleep now," Haley said, and he eased the foal onto the ground. Goldie and Sis followed him in.

Sis nursed for a while, but then she came and lay down next to the foal, her hide warm against his still damp body. "What are you going to call him, Haley? How about 'Stupid'?"

Haley laughed softly. "Brother will do for now. And don't go getting big-headed, Sis. You may be a chip off the old block, but this one probably is, too. Joe tends to throw true. And his mama may be the biggest pain in my tush we've ever had here, but she sure can run."

The foal didn't know what he meant. He fell asleep to the sound of Haley and Goldie talking softly, waking every now and then to the soft whuff-whuff of his father sniffing him.

He tried to whuff-whuff back, but was too sleepy.

Two weeks later, Brother stood out in the pasture with Goldie and Sis, watching as Lance, one of the workers on the farm, turned on a big screen set up in a way that several pastures could see it.

"Where's Haley?" Brother asked, missing the man's soft voice and gentle touch.

"Where do you think?" Sis gestured to the screen, tossing her head up so her nose and mouth pointed at it. "Dad is running in California. Haley's with him."

"Dad is running?"

Sis huffed, the way she showed sarcasm—something he'd heard way too much during his time with her and Goldie. "He's the best."

Goldie nudged her with her head, then moved away from them. "You two be quiet now. I want to watch this."

Brother wasn't sure why they had to be quiet if all she wanted to do was watch, but suddenly sound came out of the screen, and he could hear one of the two-leggers speaking, talking about the horses walking onto the track. Brother moved up to stand near Goldie, leaning against her as he watched, rapt, as his father pranced and nodded his head to the roar of the crowd when he was announced.

"He's quite the horse," Goldie murmured, nuzzling him gently.

The horses warmed up for a few minutes, then all approached a metal apparatus like the one he'd seen being pulled out to the training track on the farm. There were individual spaces for each horse, and they went into them in some kind of order that made sense to them.

"They draw for the post position," Sis said softly—he hadn't even heard her come up.

"Is his good?"

"He can win from anywhere." Sis moved closer, standing against him the way she did sometimes when she was in a really good mood. Her coat against his was soothing. "He flies out of the gate and goes to the front. It's how he races."

"He does it the same way every time? Isn't that boring?" He heard Goldie laugh. "What?"

"Don't say that to him, sweetheart. He's got how he likes to do it, and there's little chance of changing that."

"Should I run that way?"

Sis snorted. "You don't even know if you can run—in company, I mean. I've seen you do it in the field."

"And I beat you."

"Because I let you win. Didn't want to make the baby feel bad."

He huffed, and Goldie shushed them both.

He looked back at the screen, the horses were all in and suddenly the gates flew open. He saw a black blur and realized it was his father, rushing to the lead but another horse was going with him.

"Who is that?" Sis asked softly.

"If you'd paid attention to the post parade instead of fighting with your brother, you'd know."

"I don't know, either," Brother said, earning a nuzzle from Sis.

"It's Bronco. He's good. Second favorite in the betting. I'll explain that later, now shush."

Bronco was a chestnut but much darker than Goldie. He was running hard, his ears pinned back, stride for stride matching Brother's dad.

Brother wanted to ask a million things. How far did they run? How fast could his father go? Was it bad his ears were pinned back too? Would the other horses catch them if Bronco and he didn't slow down? He knew better than to bother Goldie, though.

They came to the second turn of the track—how many times did they have to go around? His dad began to pull away, a little bit at a time, but he was definitely leaving Bronco behind. Trouble was, the rest of the horses were catching up. One dark brown horse in particular was coming fast.

"Turbo," Goldie said as if she could tell he was wondering who the horse was. "He's beaten Joe once. These fractions are insane."

"Fractions?" Brother asked Sis.

"The times for the quarter miles are the fractions. She means he's going too fast."

"But if he doesn't, Bronco will pass him."

"Right. But if he does, Turbo may catch him, because he'll get tired out." Sis leaned against him. "Go, go, go."

He found himself saying the same thing as a tiring Bronco gave way to Turbo, thundering after his dad, who was clearly getting tired but wasn't giving way.

They passed a post and both slowed down as the announcer yelled, "Too close to call!"

"How do they know it's the end of the race?" Brother asked.

"The end's almost always in the same place, right in front of the stands at the wire. But the start moves depending on how long they're running and how big the track is." Goldie nudged him gently.

"You'll learn all this eventually. By doing. You don't have to understand it all now."

"But I want to. *He'll* want me to." He nodded toward the screen where his dad and Turbo were galloping out together. "Are they talking?"

"They're probably trading insults. They don't like each other."

"I don't like him, either," Sis said, sounding very sure of it.

"Me, neither," Brother said, not wanting to be left out.

"Don't dislike a horse you've never met," Goldie said, her voice stern. "It's…ignorant."

"So, you like him?"

"No, but I know him. You two don't." She stamped. "Why won't they just announce it already? Did the camera break?"

A picture flashed up on the screen, his dad's nose was just in front of Turbo's. There was a lot of noise from all the pastures and barns, and Brother asked, "How many of those screens are there?"

Goldie laughed. "When your dad decided to open his own stud farm rather than go to one of the ones owned by the two-leggers, he went a little crazy with the television access. He likes everyone to see how Runaway Farms is doing—and him in particular."

"So we have other horses running?"

"Most of the ones living here fulltime are too young to race— or retired from the game. But your father has other colts and fillies who run for a bunch of different outfits—usually wherever they were born—if they haven't worked off their foaling fee—or where they settled as free agents. Some like your sister Missive and even Flicker 'N Flight, who's not related to Joe, run for your dad because they were part of the farm he bought and turned into Runaway Farms."

Brother took this all in, trying to remember if he'd met Missive. He had a lot of brothers and sisters and it was confusing that not all of them were at the farm—even though Sis had told him that having the same dad didn't really make them brother and sister, that siblings were traditionally traced through the mom. Goldie said Joe didn't care, that he looked out for as many of his kids as he could, and that as far as she was concerned, he and Sis were brother and sister now since they shared her milk—and her.

"We watch other races, too, sometimes. The big ones, even if no one from our family or farm is running in them." Sis always seemed happy to be the font of all knowledge.

"Will we see my mother race, then?"

"You ask your dad about that." Goldie turned away.

"She races, though, right? That's why she left me here?"

"Yes," Sis said, "she's going back to the racetrack."

"Going? She's not gone yet?"

Goldie harrumphed and Sis went quiet.

"She's still here and she hasn't come to see me?"

Sis had her eyes on the screen, and Goldie nuzzled him.

"I don't understand. Why would she have me if she didn't want to be a mother?"

Goldie sighed. "It's complicated."

Sis bumped up against him gently. "If you do well as a race-horse, it'll make her worth more when she really does decide to retire."

"Sis." Goldie glared at her.

"What? It's the truth. Why keep it from him? It's only making him miserable." Sis put her head over Brother's withers. "Our dad loves you for you, though. You can run like a turtle and he won't care. You'll always have a home here." Then really softly, she said, "But I bet you'll run great. So don't worry."

He relaxed as she chewed on him lightly; it tickled in a good way. When Sis wasn't being a pain, she could be really sweet.

Brother watched as his dad made his way along the dirt row that connected the barns to the pastures. Haley and some women Brother had never seen were with him, and they seemed to be in deep conversation; none of them even glanced his way.

Sis was on the other side of the pasture, but Brother imagined if she'd been with him, their dad would have said hello.

He put his head down and wandered over to the pond pasture the yearlings preferred and then into the big turnout pasture. Goldie had told him that once upon a time fences divided all the pastures and the two-leggers had controlled everything. Now fences only ran around the perimeter of the farm, and that was to keep excited foals from racing out into the road or to keep out two-leggers and horses that didn't belong here. Other animals snuck in though. Cats and some dogs, a few goats meandered over from the neighboring farms and one of the two-leggers would take them home. The dogs usually were taken back to their homes, too, if they had one, but the cats pretty much did whatever they wanted.

Like his birth-mom, apparently.

He wandered among the older horses, nodding politely when one noticed him. There were a lot of mares, but also some free agents who had contracted with his dad to either spend some time at Runaway Farms to get over an injury or to be trained by him.

Everyone wanted a piece of his father. Brother was proud of him, even if he didn't see him very often.

He thought about that as he crested a small rise and a scent came to him, a scent that made him take deep whiffs of the gentle breeze. *She* was here. Now.

He followed his nose and saw a bay mare grazing far away from any other horses. She was damp, like she'd just gotten a bath. Probably had been training before coming out to eat.

He saw her stop eating, almost freezing, then she slowly turned around. Their eyes met and he saw welcome for a moment in hers, but as he took a step toward her, she took a step back, so he stopped.

"I'm yours," he said, and he hated how sad he sounded.

"You are." She took a step toward him, her head thrown up as if she was doing it against her will. "You smell like mine. But I'm not—"

"I know. You're going back to racing. I'm just something that might help you make more money later on." He put his head down, biting at his leg like he had an itch, not wanting to show how painful it was to be close to her when she smelled so good and looked so pretty, this horse who had carried him for eleven months and now wanted nothing to do with him. "I don't even know your name."

"Velvet Sands."

"I'm Brother right now. I don't have a name yet."

"Okay." She seemed uncomfortable, even more so than before.

He rushed to ask something else so she wouldn't leave. "Did you pick that name?"

"Yeah."

"Why?"

"I liked it." She moved closer, seemed to be studying him. "You're going to be black. Like Joe."

"I guess so." He didn't see how that was very important. "Why did you like it? Your name?"

"My best friend and I picked them, we tried to base them on where we came from—I mean long ago. Arabians and the desert."

He'd heard the foundation stories. "But the Velvet part?"

"My father's name was Serious Velvet."

"So you liked your dad? But not your mom?"

His mother suddenly turned away, muttering something about, "She had a stupid name."

"Don't go."

She didn't turn back. "Look, kid, this was great and all, but I'm leaving later tonight. I'll see you around the tracks when you grow up. Do good."

"What if I don't?"

She didn't answer, just trotted off.

He watched her go for way longer than he probably should have, then turned and saw his father standing where the pasture and the dirt road met. He threw his head up: his gesture for "Come here."

Brother walked slowly, head down—was his father going to be mad at him? Nobody wanted Brother to meet his mother. Had he broken some rule?

"Walk with me," his father said when Brother finally got to him. "And head up, you're *my* son. We can't have you looking so broken down when you're only a month old. This is the best time, no responsibilities, no worries, just grow up and have fun."

"Okay." He tried to stand a little more alertly, but he could still smell his mother—how long would the scent stay in his nose? "Why did you pick your name?" he finally asked to break the silence.

His father laughed. "Why do you think? I break out of the gate like I'm a runaway."

Brother smiled. "But the Joe part?"

"Haley's first name is Joe." He leaned down and brushed his lips across Brother's withers, a nice tickling like Sis did—had she learned it from him?

He found himself standing a little taller: his father wanted him with him.

"So you thinking about names, kiddo?"

"I guess. I have to name myself, right?"

"You have to pick names. Send a dozen or so into the place the two-leggers set up to keep track of racehorse names. And there's rules—a lot of them. Some names can't be used again, depends on what races a horse won or if they were a champion at the end of the year."

"So can another horse be Runaway Joe?"

"Nope." His father rubbed his head against Brother's neck gently. "You have plenty of time to think up names. It's your choice. I'll be there to help you and so will Haley and Goldie."

"I was thinking Black Velvet."

"That's probably taken. They don't let horses race with the same name—has to be a certain number of years between uses."

"Then Black Velvet Joe."

Joe laughed softly. "You're feeling sentimental because you just had a less than satisfactory meeting with your gem of a mother. And because you want to please me. You'll please me, Brother, don't worry about that. You give yourself a name that pleases you. If it's Black Velvet Joe, then that's fine. But maybe in time you'll find something else."

"Okay." He reached up and nuzzled his father's neck, wondering if it was okay to be the one to initiate the touching.

His father leaned into him, seemed to like the nuzzling, and said, "You're a good kid, Brother. No matter how much I dislike your mother, I'm really glad she chose me."

Brother could feel himself relaxing as he leaned against the silky black hide of his father. He saw Goldie and Sis trotting across the field, clearly looking for him. Goldie looked relieved when she saw him, and she slowed, everything about her seeming to relax. Sis sped up, reaching him first, jumping around him and vying for attention from their father.

"You had me worried, sweetheart," Goldie said when she reached him.

"He'll tell you next time before he runs off like that." His father nuzzled Goldie, as if to reassure her. "But I don't think there will be a next time quite like that. I think maybe Brother got everything he needed from today's adventure. Isn't that right, kiddo?"

"Yes, sir," Brother said, and for the first time in his short life, he quit worrying about the parent who didn't love him and realized how lucky he was to have a family who did.

No Friend Like an Old Friend

Joe stood with Haley on the backside, watching the monitors as one of his youngest two-year-olds, Long Journey, ran his first race. The colt was moving well, although he'd missed the break and was having to make up a lot of ground. But he wasn't panicking, was picking off horses, and if it had been a longer race, probably would have worked his way into the money. Unfortunately the finish line appeared before he could get himself into fourth.

"Good first effort. May need to work with him on the break, though, don't you think, Haley?"

There was no answer and Joe turned, wondering what was so important that Haley was ignoring him, and he saw his friend was sort of hunched over, holding onto his chest.

"Haley?"

"Joe, I don't feel so good." Haley reached up and grabbed Joe's mane like he was holding on for dear life. Then he started to sink down to his knees.

Wrong. Haley suddenly smelled very wrong. "Hey!" Joe yelled, and grooms and trainers came running. "Help!"

Wishing not for the first time there was a telephone made for horses, Joe nosed Haley as one of the trainers called 911.

"It'll be okay. It'll be okay," Joe said, until Haley's eyes closed and his breathing stopped and then Joe whispered, "Don't leave me," as he was pushed out of the way by a two-legger, who began CPR.

He could hear sirens and backed away as men in uniforms brought a stretcher in and carefully began to work on Haley on the ground, not putting him on the stretcher until he was breathing again.

Dead. Haley had been dead.

Joe tried to follow them to the ambulance, but one of them turned and said, "We've got this."

"He's my friend."

"We'll make sure you're called." They turned and rushed off, stopping only to get Haley into the ambulance before pulling out, lights flashing and sirens hurting his ears.

His friend was sick. His friend was dying.

He didn't know what to do.

"Did you see?" Long Journey pushed against him. "I know I missed the break but I think I could have—"

"Not now," Joe said, as he walked away from his son. He ignored the grooms and trainers and other horses, with their sympathetic eyes and wishes that meant nothing.

Haley was sick. Haley might die.

What the hell was Joe going to do?

Joe paced up and down the road between the pastures at his farm. Haley was supposedly out of the woods, but no one would let him see him. He'd gone to the hospital and been turned away. He'd tried bribing, cajoling, swearing—nothing worked. Horses weren't allowed in the hospital, and they couldn't risk bringing Haley down to see him.

If they couldn't risk bringing him out, how "out of the woods" could he be?

They'd talked on the phone, even video chatted, but Joe needed to be with him, to smell him, before he relaxed.

"You realize you're going to have to settle down, right?" A soft voice, one of the few horses willing to take him on.

He turned to face Goldie. "They won't tell me anything. Except he's out of the woods."

"I know. And I'm sorry. And frustrated too. I love Haley. We all do." She nuzzled him gently. "I'm older than you, and I was the first mare you bred to, so I'm going to say this as old woman of this farm: Haley's not just yours, Joe. All around this farm are horses who are worried sick but too afraid of you to ask how he's doing or what you know. Your kids are confused and all they see is how angry you are—they don't know that underneath it all, you're frantic."

He took a deep breath and let it out in a low frustrated neigh. "What do you want me to do?"

"Go to the track. Missive and Flicker will understand how to deal with you. And before you go, you need to talk to Long Journey: he thinks you're terribly disappointed in him."

"He ran fine first time out."

"Tell *him* that, not me." She moved closer and pressed her neck against his. "Haley will be okay."

"I don't know if he will be or not, Goldie. And it scares me to death."

"I know." With one last nuzzle, she left him alone and went back to where Sis and Brother waited, both watching him more nervously than he liked.

He told the driver to get the van ready to head back to the track. He made a point of walking the farm before he left, putting on a calm he didn't really feel, telling the older horses what he knew, trying to put his younger foals at ease.

He got to where Long Journey was grazing and walked over. "I'm sorry."

"For what? I screwed up the break. I get it. I let you down."

"You didn't. And it's an easy mistake to make when you're first starting out. I'll work with you once Haley gets back. Other than the break, you ran a great race. Maybe pick a bit longer race next time. You need the room to get in stride. I think you would have caught them if you'd been going seven furlongs instead of five and a half."

Long Journey seemed to be perking up with each word. "Good idea. And thanks."

Joe nosed him, not the way he would his younger foals, because Long Journey was a typical two-year-old and didn't want to be embarrassed by too much affection. "I'll be at the track if you need me."

"Okay. Thank you."

"Don't thank me, son. I'm sorry I blew you off."

Gray Dawn listened for the normal cocky good humor that seemed to emanate from Joe's part of the barns. But everyone was subdued. Even Flicker seemed to be somber when he should be still riding high after his Derby win or nervous for the Preakness this weekend.

Gray stopped at his stall and murmured, "What's going on?"

Flicker motioned for Gray to walk with him away from Joe's corner of the track and didn't talk until they were well clear of all the barns. "Haley had a heart attack."

"Crap. I didn't hear about that." This is what he got for going on his self-promotion tour—and leaving Deirdre, his main link to racetrack news and gossip, with Mister Moss. "Is he going to be okay? He's not dead, is he?"

"He's alive, but they're not big with the info. Haley was always our conduit for that. And now he's in a hospital, and Joe's going crazy and taking it out on anyone who makes the mistake of, well, breathing." Flicker pawed the ground. "I'm not a big fan of Joe's, but I am of Haley. He's been good to me. And he loves Joe. I just wish there were a way for Joe to see him. If he knew Haley was in good hands and he'll come home, I think he would settle down."

"Why can't he see him?"

"Gray, it's a hospital. A two-legger hospital. A horse can't just stroll into one. And believe me, Joe tried. But they said hospital policy or something—I don't know but he came back more pissed than when he left."

Gray began to laugh—a devious sound and Flicker looked at him in surprise. "Just so happens my girl Safe Haven has a rather interesting fellow working for her. Kevin—you've met him, right?"

"Yeah, Missive likes him. I've been over with her to hang out with your daughter."

His daughter. He almost sighed. He knew he'd let her down if a father like Joe was what she wanted. But if she needed help, he'd move heaven and Earth to get it to her. She didn't know that, though, and he hoped she was never in enough trouble to need to find out.

"Well, my fine Derby-winning friend." He saw Flicker preen just a bit and bobbed his head—someone should be giving the kid his props for winning, even if there was other stuff going on. "Kevin just happens to have friends in high places—and low ones. All sorts of levels from what I can tell. Why don't we go see if there's any way he can help us get Joe into that hospital?"

Flicker started to laugh. "Oh, man, how much is he going to hate it that it's *us* helping him out?"

"Will make the good deed all the sweeter, I admit." With another slightly evil laugh, Gray led him the long way around the barns to get to his shedrow. No sense in running into Joe until they knew if they could get this done.

Joe fidgeted as Kevin put the rubber cups over his hooves. "Why am I wearing these again?"

"Because hospital floors are hard and the clippy-clop of Joe-sized hooves is going to be a dead giveaway." He took them off again, spritzing them down with antibacterial spray. "Germs and all. We'll put these on when you get there. You don't need to be picking up any weird microbes and stuff here."

Joe had a sudden vision of this tough-talking guy as a complete germaphobe. The image made him happy, if only for a moment.

Kevin didn't seem to notice. "So my guy is taking you up the freight elevator, but you still have to get into Haley's room. Damn good thing he's out of ICU, or we'd never pull this off."

Joe wasn't sure he really liked this Kevin guy. But Gray and Flicker had suggested he could help, and Gray trusted the guy with his daughter, so he must be all right. Then again Gray was one of the worst dads Joe had ever seen, so maybe that wasn't much of an endorsement.

"Okay, I'll get the van. We're using a rental so no one will add two and two together and get Runaway Farms." Kevin went off with Flicker, who seemed to think he was in charge of "Operation Visit Haley."

Joe muttered, "His head's nearly bigger than his stall door after winning the Derby."

"Not winning. Romping. He won by six lengths. You could congratulate him, you know." Gray helped himself to some hay, and when Joe shot him a glare, he said, "What? Scheming makes me peckish."

"I know why he might want to get in my good graces since he's head over hooves for my girl. But why the hell are you stepping up, Gray?" Joe listened for the sound of the van as he waited.

"Because I owe you for the advice about the farm. Dawn Enterprises is going to be amazing. We'll give you a run for your money."

Joe snorted. That would be the day.

Gray's expression changed, all bluster dropping away. "But mostly I think of Deirdre. It killed me to let her go away for the summer with Mister Moss and that monster he calls a cat. I can't even imagine what I would do if she got sick. So that's why I'm helping." He moved a little closer. "And if you need anything—and I mean that sincerely—just ask."

Joe found himself more touched than he wanted to be, so he shook his head to keep the emotion from taking him over the way it had at the farm. Goldie had been right. He'd been making everyone miserable because he was so upset over Haley—over not knowing how bad it was. "Thank you," he finally said.

"You're welcome. Now, let's go break you into the hospital."

They walked out to where Kevin had parked the nondescript van, and Joe climbed in. Flicker stood close to Gray, as if he was getting moral support from the old guy. Figured: Gray was a better dad to a horse he hadn't sired than one he had.

But he was right. Flicker had romped and Joe should be nicer to him: if not for Missive's sake then to keep him interested in retiring to Runaway Farms when he was done racing.

"Hey, lightweight," Joe said to Flicker, watching the colt go up on his toes the way he always did when Joe used that particular insult. "Damn fine race. I've been remiss in saying that. Don't let them psyche you out in the Preakness."

"I won't. I leave this afternoon so I guess I'll hear from Missive how Haley is."

"Or I'll call you. Least I can do after you planned this big caper."

Flicker pranced a little, shifting in the pretty way that was earning him fans on the track for how he danced. "It was mostly Gray's idea."

"Well, whoever was the big mastermind, I appreciate it." Before things could get any mushier, Joe told Kevin to close the door and get this show on the road.

Which he immediately regretted. Kevin's driving left something to be desired. Joe moved to the opening that allowed horses to talk to the driver, and said, "Are you aiming for every pothole?"

"Shitty old van, Your Majesty. Drives like crap. Now could you try to stay hidden? We're almost there."

Joe did as he asked, and Kevin gave him a running commentary of "Okay, we're pulling in. Driving out back to the delivery area—nope, gotta wait, uniform people are here with delivery. I'm texting Manuel—okay, he's on his way down."

Kevin got out of the driver's seat and came around back, climbing into the van and getting the rubber hoof caps in place. "You are one big horse, buddy. I have no idea if this is going to work."

"It has to."

"Right, well, if you're a praying horse, you might want to phrase whatever you ask God for as a request and not an order. You seem kind of entitled."

Joe closed his eyes, ready to pray for patience with two-leggers who thought now was a good time to lecture him on his character.

A younger man walked up and Kevin introduced him as Manuel.

"Come on," Manuel said, his voice quiet and full of a sweetness Joe found comforting. "I gotta tell you, I'm a huge fan of yours. But…I'm going to lose my job if we're caught."

"I'll say I forced you."

Manuel laughed, a sharp bark of amusement that he cut off. "I doubt they'd listen. So, be careful, seriously, because I'm supporting a family."

Joe liked that; it was clear the kid cared about his family. "And I have a lot of freaking money. If you lose your job, I will make sure you land on your feet until you find a new job—or you can come work for me. Whatever works best."

Manuel touched his neck, a surprisingly ballsy move, but all Joe could sense from him was respect and affection. "Haley's been asking about you."

"Yeah?"

"Yeah. I think he's going as crazy as you are." Manuel pushed the button for the freight elevator, and Joe thought he heard him murmuring, "Please be empty, please be empty, please be empty."

It was empty, and Joe followed him on, riding the quick trip to the fifth floor—this time he found himself repeating Manuel's litany as the door opened to the corridor. "Please be empty, please be empty, please be empty."

It was. "Hurry," Manuel said, and Joe walked quickly after him, his rubber-clad feet making virtually no noise. He had to duck to get into the door Manuel held open for him, and then he saw him.

Haley.

Sitting up and looking bored as hell.

"Slacking off as usual," Joe said, and he didn't try to keep the relief and happiness out of his voice.

Haley turned, a huge grin splitting his face. "What the hell, Joe? You aren't supposed to be in here—that's what they told me."

"Yeah, well, you know me and rules." Joe moved closer, whiffing as soon as he was near enough, getting a sense for how Haley smelled, how healthy he was. The wrong smell was gone. His scent was normal Haley, if also strong with hospital smells.

"Knock it off, boss. I'm good as gold. Just had to get some arteries cleaned out. Nothing big." He shifted and Joe could tell the movement caused him pain.

"Sure, nothing big."

"I'm going to keep watch in the hall," Manuel said, and slipped out the door.

"Nice kid," Joe said.

"He is. I like him." Haley reached up, again wincing with the movement.

Joe stepped closer, eased his head down so Haley could touch him, then let it drop softly into Haley's lap, holding it there, content to just "be" with his old friend. "I was so afraid you were going to die."

"You and me both, Joe." Haley sniffed. "And I wasn't going to get to see you before I went. I hated that." He rubbed Joe's neck softly. "One of us is going to go first, you know?"

"We'll live forever, Haley. That's my plan." Joe lifted his head and met Haley's eyes. "Honestly, I figured it'd be me going first. I never imagined having to live without you. I'm not sure I know how to."

"'Course you do. You're the smartest horse I know. Nothing ever stands in your way." He slipped his fingers through Joe's mane. "Doesn't mean I want you to have to do it on your own. I'll be back. Just going to take a while to recuperate."

"Anything you need, I'll get. Hell, I'll hire Manuel away if you want him to be your private nurse."

Haley started to laugh, then winced again and said, "Damn it, Joe, don't make me laugh." He took a couple of deep breaths, then said, "Manuel works in the IT department. He only came up here to talk to me because he's such a fan of yours. And I don't need a nurse. I just need to get well. They'll give me rules and exercises and dietary instructions that are going to piss me off. But other than that, I'll be fine." He rubbed Joe's nose. "This has always felt like velvet to me. Ever since you were a baby."

"I never had a dad."

"Every horse has a dad, Joe. You never had an *involved* dad."

"Fine, but what I mean is you were my dad. And maybe if I'm a good dad, it's because of you. How you treated me. The interest you took in all of us."

"But you, mostly. You don't see me working for any of your brothers or sisters do you?"

"Nyah. But why would you? They're not me." Joe laughed and for the first time since Haley had collapsed, he felt real happiness.

They stood in silence, Joe breathing easily, feeling all the parts of him that had been so uptight finally calming down as Haley rubbed his nose and leaned back, closing his eyes.

Manuel told him it was time to go before he was ready. But it was okay now. Haley would be home eventually.

Joe settled in on the grass in Haley's favorite pasture. He'd had Manuel drive Haley over in one of the farm carts.

Manuel hadn't lost his job, but Joe had lured him over to the farm when he found out Manuel wasn't just an IT tech but a bit of a computer whiz kid. His new project, when he wasn't ferrying Haley around during his recuperation, was coming up with a phone horses could use.

It was going to make him rich. Joe would do nicely too as a major investor. Even Gray and Mister Moss had gone in as backers. Seemed like a lot of horses were sick of relying on two-leggers to maintain communication.

"Okay, settle him down easy," Joe said, and Manuel rolled his eyes and murmured, "I've done this like a hundred times."

"Exaggeration will get you nowhere," Haley said as he shifted so he was leaning comfortably against Joe's shoulder. "I've only been home two weeks."

"The best two weeks of my life," Joe murmured, not caring that Manuel heard the fondness—the utter sappiness, if Joe was honest. Manuel was a good kid and he'd already asked Joe a lot of questions about what he wanted his phones to do, going into details Joe never would have thought about.

"Okay, I'll be back in an hour with meds, Haley." Manuel drove off, navigating carefully.

"He drives like a little old lady," Haley said, laughing softly. "But he's a good kid."

"He is. I like him."

Haley got quiet and leaned up against Joe firmly, the way they'd been doing now since he got back. Just enjoying this beautiful piece of Kentucky, the sound of horses training and simply being themselves.

"So he drove me past the south pasture on the way here."

"Mmm hmmm." Joe had been waiting for this convo.

"You're walling off part of it?"

"I'm making a cemetery." He turned his head so he could see Haley's expression. "One of us is going to die first. There could be accidents for other horses associated with the farm. We need a final resting place. 'Course I'm assuming you haven't made alternate plans when I say 'we.'"

"When have I ever had an alternate plan where you're concerned?" Haley moved his head so his face was against Joe's neck. "Where you gonna stick me? In the back with the weeds?"

Joe laughed but tried not to move too much; he didn't want to disturb Haley. "Yep, in some crappy spot." He let that sit for a moment, then said more softly, "Actually, it's right next to my spot. It's the highest part of the space. I thought...I mean we founded this place. We should have the places of honor, right? Together."

Haley was really quiet and Joe waited, but all he could feel from him was a small sense of distress they had to talk about this and love—so much love. "Together sounds great, Joe," he finally said.

"Unless I fire you first." Their old joke. One Joe had not used till now, not when he hadn't been sure he wasn't going to lose Haley.

Haley pressed his face tighter against Joe, his hand coming up to stroke him gently. "Right...if you don't fire me first."

About the Author

Gerri Leen has been obsessed with horse racing since she was a girl, growing up in the Seattle area inhaling the Black Stallion novels, going to Longacres with her mother and aunt, and riding at western horse camp on the weekends. Now retired in Northern Virginia, she still follows racing avidly. She writes both poetry and prose and also romance as Kim Strattford.

Her works have appeared in *The Magazine of Fantasy and Science Fiction*, *Strange Horizons*, *Dark Matter*, *Escape Pod*, *Zooscape*, and others. In 2024, she published her first poetry collection *Unwilling: Poems of Horror and Darkness* and a fiction collection *The Woman I Used to Be and Other Speculative Imaginings*. Her poetry has been nominated for the Pushcart Prize as well as the Rhysling and Dwarf Stars awards.

You can find more at gerrileen.com. This is her first novel.

More Books from
WolfSinger Publications

Midnight Menagerie – edited by Carol Hightshoe

Step right up, dear traveler—your ticket to the extraordinary awaits.

Beneath the striped canopies of the *Midnight Menagerie*, wonders stir and nightmares awaken. Strongmen flex their might, fortune tellers spin futures, and acrobats defy the stars. But if it is shadows you seek—if you are drawn to the hush of velvet-draped corners where the line between spectacle and sorcery blurs—then step closer.

Here, within these pages, beasts from beyond the veil prowl in cages not quite strong enough. Carnival performers barter in secrets instead of silver. Mystics weave illusions that refuse to fade, and every whispered promise carries a cost. From the neon glow of alien menageries to the flickering lantern light of haunted carnivals, *Midnight Menagerie* is a collection of the eerie, the wondrous, and the strange.

So take your seat, dear reader. The lights are dimming, the curtains are rising… and the show is about to begin.

The World of the Moho – Tyree Campbell

Aldon (Allie) McIntyre, a white American geologist with a thirst for adventure, and Thadie Mayane, a Black South African mining supervisor with a commanding presence, are exploring the depths of an abandoned mine when the floor collapses, hurling them into an extraordinary realm known as Below. Nestled between the Earth's crust and mantle, this vast world is home to breathtaking landscapes, intelligent species—some friendly, others predatory—and dangers unlike anything they've ever imagined.

Forced to rely on each other for survival, Allie and Thadie must navigate treacherous terrain, fend off alien predators, and face the looming threat of capture by those who see them as little more than slaves. As they search for the legendary passage back to Above, their uneasy alliance will be tested by the perilous environment—and the prejudices and mistrust they each carry.

Will they overcome the trials of Below and find their way back Above? Or will this stunning and dangerous world consume them entirely—if they don't destroy each other first?

Mars in Carnage – William Paul Lazarus

Humanity's dream of colonizing Mars quickly becomes a fight for survival. Mission director Lt Col. John Hathaway sends astronauts Aadya "Kate" Khatun and Hamza "Arti" Artsruni to explore and establish a foothold on the Red Planet. One astronaut is killed, during what appears to be an alien attack; the other makes a solo, dangerous return to a hero's welcome on Earth.

Over a century later a Martian colony has firmly established— the underground city of Katarti, Cecil Townley, a tour guide for visitors to Mars is captured by a band of terrorists trying to end what they believe are horrible governmental actions on Mars. Hiding in underground tunnels, they begin their attack with Townley forced to be their guide. Their actions introduce him to a world he never knew existed, far from the innocent tale he had been telling newcomers for years.

Cowboy Up – edited by Carol Hightshoe

Cowboy Up gathers stories that celebrate the timeless tradition of rodeo. The dust, the grit, the glory—it's all here.

From the echoes of the past to the rodeo arenas of today, these stories will take you on a wild ride through the highs and lows of rodeo life. You'll share in their triumphs and their heartbreaks. From the unbreakable bond between rider and horse to the courage it takes to get back in the saddle after a fall, this anthology is a tribute to the spirit that keeps rodeo alive.

But this book isn't just about telling stories. It's about giving back. Eighty-Five percent of proceeds from Cowboy Up will be donated to the Justin Cowboy Crisis Fund, a non-profit organization dedicated to helping injured rodeo athletes get back on their feet. Your purchase helps support those who risk it all in the arena, offering them a lifeline when they need it most.

So saddle up. Dive into these tales of resilience, heart, and the cowboy way. With every story, you're not just reading about rodeo —you're helping to keep its spirit alive.

Homefall Search – Dana Bell

Charged with finding the best place for a new Homefall, Jehna Talon searched on Saris, a world located in the Tashiti Nebula. Along with her Arial shapeshifter companions, she goes into the Ghost Mountains to find a specific valley, only to become trapped during a storm and encounters a native dragon.

With local rancher Harrison Talbot she negotiates the price for the land. Brides, for him and his hands. As her uncle taught her, there's always a need to be filled. Traveling to Aris and with the help of a local contact, she finds women willing to brave the frontiers of space.

Returning to Ronia, home of the Talons, she learns opposition from the other clan leaders may stop the dream she had of becoming a clan leader. They argue there are too few Rovers, and she'll never succeed.

Could they be right, despite her already finding the ideal location?

The Dragon's Hoard 3 – edited by Carol Hightshoe

In this anthology, twenty-six authors weave enchanting stories of dragons—from the fierce and fire-breathing to the wise and benevolent. Enter a treasure trove of tales where dragons reign supreme and hoards are more than mere gold.

Discover hidden gems of wisdom and magic within these lairs. Feast on tales that shimmer with magic, adventure, and the timeless allure of dragons. Explore the myriad treasures dragons hold dear and the legends that surround them.

From heartwarming tales of friendship and loyalty to thrilling adventures filled with danger and magic, these tales offer something for every dragon lover. Whether they are guardians of treasure, seekers of knowledge, or forces of nature: the dragons in this collection will ignite your imagination.

The Dragon's Hoard 2 – edited by Carol Hightshoe

Welcome to realms where dragons reign, treasures abound, and every adventure leads to magic. Explore stories that spark the imagination and might just awaken the dragon within. Are you brave enough to face the dragon and claim your prize?

From the unyielding grip of ancient magics to the cunning of those who seek dragons, their treasure or both—each story weaves a rich tapestry of magic and lore.

Whether it's a battle for survival, the forging of an unlikely alliance, or a humorous twist on hoarding habits, our authors invite you to delve into realms where dragons not only hoard gold but also secrets, spells, and sometimes, even friendships. After all, in the world of dragons, not all treasures are silver and gold—some are stories waiting to be told.

The Hounds of Ardagh – Laura J Underwood

Ginny Ni Cooley never desired more than the simple life she had, living in Tamhasg Wood and using her magic to occasionally assist the folk of Conorscroft while putting up with the machinations of the ghost of her former mentor Manus MacGreeley. But her peace is shattered one night with the arrival of a lad who is fleeing a pack of red-gold hounds led by a hound-shaped demon known as Nidubh.

So much for peace and solitude. By rescuing Fafne MacArdagh, Ginny becomes wrapped in the fabric of an intrigue involving a family feud, a traitorous son, and a blood mage named Edain who is determined to keep her soul. It is she who cast a spell on Fafne's family and household and transformed the MacArdaghs into hounds.

Ginny gives Fafne her word to take him to Caer Keltora so they can report the matter to the Council of Mageborn. But Edain is determined to keep her secret and her soul intact and moves to thwart Ginny at every turn.

For Ginny Ni Cooley who has faced many bogies, dealing with a demon, a bloodmage and the Dark Lord of Annwn will be no easy task. But she will do what she must to undo Edain's spells. If not, Manus' soul will become part of Arawn's Cauldron of Doom. Ginny will become a demon's feast, and poor Fafne will join the Hounds of Ardagh.

Wee Folk and Wise: A Fairies Anthology

– edited by Deby Fredericks

All over the world, fairy tales are told.
There are big fairies and little fairies.
Ugly fairies and pretty fairies.
Wise fairies and silly fairies.
Sweet fairies and scary fairies.

Seventeen authors share their own fantastic fairy tales in this magical collection. What kind of fairy will you meet here?

Infinity – Ted Pennella

In the distant future, when peace between humanity and the artificial intelligences their ancestors created has been settled, Conrad Conner tries to live a quiet and unassuming life in orbit about Jupiter on the city-station Socrates' Odyssey. When Conner's attempt to create a prototypical communication artificial for use by the Sol-Humana Confederation's Stellar Fleet gets derailed by the attempted murder of the very artificial he's created, his life spirals into a mad flight back to Earth to try and save at least his sister's children, if not his sister herself. Past failures and heartaches resurface as seemingly unconnected dots become a plot by the First Admiral to steal not just power over the Confederation, but a secret Conner holds within himself.

A secret not even Conner knows about.

Flatlanders - Mike Sherer

Young theoretical physicist Mickey Haiku has fallen into Eden's trap. She is a much smarter scientist who is intent on saving her own dimension by destroying his. Unbeknownst to either, beings from several yet higher dimensions have their own strategies. This sends the mixed-up pawns off on a wild odyssey through a dozen weird, twisted dimensions. As if this hyper-dimensional odyssey isn't challenging enough for Mickey, he has the additional difficulty of embarking on this whacko tour as a (pregnant!) female. Which means Eden is stuck in Mickey's body. The two are soon forced to cooperate since each holds the other's body hostage.

The strangest relationship this side of the 11th dimension

develops between the two.

And more – check out our books at
www.wolfsingerpubs.com